UNDER THE
WINDMILLS

*To Leita —
Enjoy the book!
Regards —
Cindy*

D1158796

a novel

UNDER THE WINDMILLS

CINDY M. CALLINS

TATE PUBLISHING
AND ENTERPRISES, LLC

Published by Tate Publishing & Enterprises, LLC
127 E. Trade Center Terrace | Mustang, Oklahoma 73064 USA
1.888.361.9473 | www.tatepublishing.com

Tate Publishing is committed to excellence in the publishing industry. The company reflects the philosophy established by the founders, based on Psalm 68:11,
"The Lord gave the word and great was the company of those who published it."

Published in the United States of America

ISBN: 978-1-61777-344-0
1. Fiction / Westerns
2. Fiction / Romance / Suspense
11.12.01

CHAPTER ONE

Windmills
Early sun cranks windmill gears
To churn and shape the sky,
Invading earth beneath the ground to water what the
sun bakes dry.
Metal looms above the ground hiding labor's quest.
Engine gears pick up the slack when hot sun forces rest.
Ranches reap the tower's work with water far below,
Praise obtrusive metal designed to help earth grow.
Definition of the sky through hills and on the plains,
Invented as defense against the summer's lack of rain.

The day was already quite hot, typical of what the Texas sun had to offer in the summer to anyone who dared challenge its mood in midafternoon. Today, the Straight S Ranch was having its monthly tack, hay, and miscellaneous farm sale on the empty lot of a main thoroughfare in one of the few nearby cities, Benning. It was sort of a tradition for all the ranch hands, their wives, children, or anyone interested in packing up a truck or maybe pulling a horse trailer to offer dollar pony rides to the wide-eyed city kids while the hands lay in the sun waiting for the curious and inexperienced to purchase their goods.

But for all who were involved in the sale it was actually loads of fun. Everybody watched everybody else's stuff so the cowboys and their families could take turns eating at a local restaurant or shopping at the Walmart, something they couldn't normally do living so far from town. The workers loved to linger and enjoy the day knowing they didn't have to feed chickens, water an animal, or load hay for one joyous, lazy afternoon. After all, they were making extra money by selling their homemade farm tack and goods. Surely a handmade lead rope would be perfect in a city boy's room hanging on the wall next to a rock idol.

There was no comparing life in the city to that of the life which existed on the Straight S Ranch and all the hands were aware of that fact as they gossiped, griped, laughed, and spread tales any intelligent person knew could not possibly be true. Today, though, these people morphed into a different world on this barren, hot lot—a world they couldn't wait to escape to once a month, yet one they were itching to leave at the end of the day.

Sally stretched out on some hay bales in the shade while a batch of Blue Heeler pups curled up beside her, a cardboard sign supporting one of the sleeping dogs. It was her third time to come into town with the ranch hands to indulge in every lazy moment the day had to offer. Being the daughter of the Straight S's head foreman meant there was always a chore to be completed. At least for one day out of the month she could drive away from the land that demanded every minute of her time and—even though the life of the ranch accompanied her—she thanked God the chores did not. But after the partying and dancing at dusk she knew no one would be physically capable to give a hundred percent the next day and her work would double until everyone acclimated to the familiar routine of ranch life. Nothing in life was free. It was a good day, even though her thoughts were constantly fettered with unanswered questions and her spirit possessed a restlessness that seared her soul from the moment she woke up until the time she fell asleep from exhaustion.

A hot, southern breeze swept across her face blowing her long, sweaty, sixties hair in every direction. Her right boot caught a baling wire and she pushed herself up, a shiny gold clip clasping the outlaw hair. Sally loved the country life even though three months earlier she had balked about leaving New Orleans where she was living with her aunt while she attended Louisiana University. She had relocated to New Orleans five long years ago when her parents insisted she pack up and live with Aunt Lucille. Sally hadn't wanted to leave the ranch in the first place, but then when she finally secured relationships and established herself socially (which means she knew where the Starbucks was located) in New Orleans, her father adamantly insisted she return to Texas.

Sally's dad was the head of ten foremen on one of the oldest and largest ranches in the Southwest. He specifically oversaw the breeding and raising of the cattle, a position he had held for the past twenty-two years—exactly Sally's age. He attributed his wrinkles and dark, leather skin to the harsh sun and walked bowlegged— the result of riding and breaking horses his whole life. His joints ached constantly, the natural result of wrestling cattle, roping calves, mending fences, and desperately trying to control an uncontrollable land. John never complained about anything, but, after her mother's death, clearly it was Sally's duty to return to the ranch and help out her dad, physically and emotionally. So when he insisted she return she felt compelled and obligated, but as the days edged closer to come home she felt Texas—not just her dad—pulling her back to an uncertain and mysterious life.

That morning, at the ranch, Sally saw a friend, a dear friend she cherished from an uncertain childhood. She'd been home for three months before she caught a glimpse of him from a distance. Although he was sixteen years older than Sally, she viewed him as ageless as he had once been her salvation at a time in life when salvation did not seem possible. Over the last five years of Sally's absence he somehow managed to acquire massive amounts of acreage. A land baron in Texas these days was certainly the result of an inheritance from a long-gone era—someone else's hard-fought legacy. But Adam somehow created his own legacy in a time when money persuaded and land demanded money.

Perspiration accumulated on Sally's chest as she realized a degree in art was not a fair combative tool compared to Adam's land acquisitions. She would be at a disadvantage when they finally met up again, which made her edgy and suspicious of the man who contributed to her maturity and formation into womanhood. Modern society convinced her that no one these days could just buy up large portions of land without the pervasion of some kind of underhanded dealings, but Adam had made a difference in her life at one time and that constituted loyalty and trust first and foremost.

While Sally struggled through the awkward years Adam yielded his time and sympathy. Sally's mind drifted back to her junior high days, sparking a pang of self-pity while remembering the cruelty of her classmates. When her classmates insisted she have the end-of-the-year party at her house, Sally had basked in her newfound acceptance. She and her mother uncharacteristically spent happy days cleaning the house and preparing for her friends. They cooked and created hot dips and finger foods. But the night of the party arrived and no one showed up, not even Sally's best friend. It was a cruel, adolescent joke at Sally's expense. But Adam rode out to the pasture where she had escaped and handed back to Sally the dignity and pride her thoughtless junior high classmates had stripped away in only one short night. Guilt invaded her spirit, wiping away jealous, suspicious, and resentful thoughts of a friend who justified her existence at age thirteen.

But at times Sally felt validation of her jealousy toward Adam when her father's attitude fettered her everyday existence. He often became furious and then indifferent when she mentioned her dreams and aspirations about owning her own ranch, undermining her confidence as her classmates had so long ago. And thoughts of Aunt Lucille's mysterious departure at the airport when she said she wished she had the courage to explain why her dad had insisted Sally live with her haunted her daily routine and thoughts. The comfortable base she used to call home before she left for New Orleans did not exist anymore.

Sally closed her eyes from mental exhaustion. The laughter of the crowd blended in with the passing of the cars, the stomping of the horses, and the shallow breathing of the pups curled beside her. The unique combination of sounds mesmerized her soul as she drifted off under the shade of the mesquite trees, a welcome sabbatical from her troubled and confusing thoughts. Some parts of Texas did provide relief.

"Excuse me, are you selling these Heelers?" An obtrusive voice interrupted Sally's serenity as one of the pups accidentally fell off a square bale of hay as she tried to quickly sit up. Its pathetic yelp brought immediate attention from the man.

"Come on, little fella, you're all right." The empathy was apparent, the voice evoking memories of Sally's youth—a voice she once relied on to survive. The man scooped up the dog and held it near his chest, allowing the vibrating pup to absorb a steady heartbeat. "I think I made a friend."

The sun partially blinded Sally's vision although she did not need her eyes to conclude it was Adam who was standing in front of her. He leaped on the back of the truck with the pup cupped in his hand.

"Aren't you going to speak to an old friend?" her hero and nemesis asked.

All Sally could see at this moment was the man she remembered from her junior high and high school days, a gentle refuge from the teenage years. His deep, blue eyes still reached out to her soul even though his sweat-stained hat covered his forehead and shadowed his face. "Adam, I haven't spoken with you in such a long time." Sally leaned forward and ceremoniously hugged the man. Adam kissed her on the cheek.

"I rode out to the Straight S this morning and saw you and your caravan of ranch hands heading for the city."

"Yeah, you know the monthly tack sale. My dad told me yesterday you were coming over this morning to buy a bull from him."

"I was hoping to talk to you while I was there. You look good." Adam shifted his weight, still holding the pup while staring into the moving crowd. "I thought it might be nice to go for a bite to eat and catch up."

Sally followed his gaze to the open field. "Okay. I'd like that. I guess we could catch up on the last five years." Sally lovingly petted the dog in Adam's hand. "Do you want the pup?"

"How long are you going to be in town?" Adam asked, somewhat distracted.

Sally slowly removed the squirming puppy from Adam's hands. "Until after the dance." Sally's eyes once again gazed at the crowd. She envied the relaxed movements of the townspeople sauntering about happily in the grassy fields. A young dad was protectively keeping pace alongside a pony as his son enjoyed an afternoon ride. A teenage girl from the ranch was explaining how to care for a rabbit she was about to sell as it wriggled nervously in her hands. The wind spread the happy voices throughout the fields and into the branches of the mesquite trees.

"How about getting that bite to eat before the dance?"

Sally turned toward Adam. "Somehow I knew I would be talking to you today. Is this a rescue mission?"

"A rescue mission?"

Sally jumped down from the truck gate onto the dusty ground. "You know," she said suspiciously, "I haven't seen you for about five years; I've been back home for over three months—which I'm sure you knew—and now we're sitting here acting like we're familiar neighbors. Why did you wanna know how long I was going to be in town?"

"I wanted to know how long you were going to be in town because I wanted to ask you out to eat. Something going on?"

"Naww. I guess I just find it funny to talk so casually after five years of not seeing each other."

"I understand… Well, I guess I'm not good at breaking the ice. Let's head out."

"Sure." Sally searched for conversation. "I heard you won a district seat. Wow, a politician on top of everything else! How do you find the time with your ranch and all?"

"Let's talk over food. I'm starved."

"I'd love to talk about your district seat and all the other things you've accomplished while I've been away." Sally found herself floundering in her own words with the need to be formal and distant.

"My truck is next to the hay wagon; you go on ahead. I'll be right along." Adam slipped away while Sally corralled the reluctant pups back in their cage and secured a ranch hand to sell them for her. She stared at the helpless dogs keenly. They'll be gone by the time I get back, she thought sadly. She climbed into Adam's truck and slammed the door, immediately rolling down the window and propping her boots on the dashboard as her mind drifted to the past once again.

Adam had rallied for her in her youth when John stayed busy with the ranch and her mother never quite seemed interested in a young girl's teenage life. He filled in the blanks, replenishing her life with laughter and acceptance. But her feelings about Adam changed when she entered high school. She felt anger toward him deep inside and, even though he sensed it, Adam accepted her feelings with patience. A young girl's feelings change in high school, and Sally was not sure the role he had so often played in her life was the same relationship she wanted to continue. Her only response was confusion and frustration with no avenue open to explore. He had never been anything but giving to her and now she realized the anger was still present. Time had not changed much between them.

Adam reached the truck, puppy in hand. He smiled and jumped into the driver's seat, setting the plump little dog in Sally's lap. "I decided fate landed this little fellow in my lap. Cute, isn't he?"

Sally raised the pup with both hands as it greedily licked her cheek. He smelled of a newborn puppy and the more he licked her face, the more he wagged his tail. Again, Sally felt that sadness as she looked into the puppy's eyes. She fed and cared for this dog six long weeks and now for money he's going to belong to someone else. "You gonna train it to run cattle?" she asked, diverting a wet tongue from her new acquisition.

"Don't know. I need a pup around the house. Lost my other one to coyotes a while back."

"You say it so casually. Animals are important, you know."

"Time does heal, and life goes on. Where would you like to go?"

Sally peered above the dashboard at the host of people once again. "I shouldn't venture very far from the bunch."

"They're just here to have a good time. I don't think they need a keeper."

"I don't know. I'm supposed to make sure nothing goes wrong."

"We'll only be gone for a little while. We'll be back for the dance tonight, I promise."

Satisfied, Sally turned her attention toward Adam. "I've never seen you at one of these get-togethers. Scoping out the competition for Hamilton Ranch?"

"Think I need to steal ranch hands from you?"

"I don't know. Do you?"

"Hardly."

"Speaking of hands, why don't the families from Hamilton Ranch ever have a tack sale? I've never seen any of your workers come into town. Everyone from the Straight S loves it and it gives them a chance to leave the ranch for a while. I think they enjoy all the city people; it makes them feel important, explaining what everything is and how to care for the animals people buy, telling those exaggerated, glorified stories of ranch life."

"That aren't so exaggerated at times." Adam started up the engine. "I guess most of my hands are caught up in the rodeo. I have several boys who will probably go professional soon, though I hate to lose them to a one-in-a-million shot of making it in the pro circuit. A while back they put up a pen on the east side of the ranch and made some chutes. They're out there every evening trying to kill themselves."

"You don't approve? I think it's exciting. I adore the rodeo. You take chances and risks you normally wouldn't take and the crowd loves it! They scream and clap and cheer you on. I've been putting in my time for the barrel-racing event. I just sent in my rookie application for the Abilene rodeo at the end of the summer."

"But you're not giving up your livelihood to do it full-time. They're just dreamers and fools."

"Aren't we all at one time or another in our lives?"

As the two were riding along, Sally spoke above the wind from the open windows. "I can't help but think there is something a bit unusual about your timely dinner invitation. Even though I like the thought of spending the afternoon together with an old friend, I can't help but wonder if history is repeating itself. Did my father ask you to come and see me today?"

"I bought the finest bull from your dad today. We're working on some breeding…"

"I don't think that answers my question."

"What do you want to know? I came into town and asked you out to eat because I thought we'd catch up and have a laugh about some great memories. You still want to go?"

"Sure."

"Name the place then."

Sally stared at Adam for a while as the truck drove down Main Street, the uneven road forcing repetitive sounds from the tires resembling a train racing down the track. "I don't know. A hamburger and fries sounds good."

"How about the drive-in? Too hot for you to sit in the truck and eat?"

"No. I like the drive-in. Tell me about your district seat. I was surprised when I heard you held a public office. I didn't know you were interested in politics."

"Interested in politics? No. Interested in the welfare of my ranch and other ranches in the area? Yes. It was necessary for everyone's well-being around here to petition a redistricting, which included the larger ranches. There were too many diverse problems and too many people widespread to fairly represent all the issues the way it was originally divided. The area is really growing, and with that comes diversity. It took a while; I fought the Democrats and Republicans on this one. I was lucky it had been ten years since the last redistricting. I had to wait for a favorable team of state judges to rule on my proposal for boundary changes, and I had to assure the Native American, Hispanic, German, Czech—you get the picture— population that I was the one to best represent them... I probably submitted as many papers to Congress as you did in your college career, but it all worked out eventually and I won the district seat."

"Well, you've sized that up in a neat little packet. I'm sure there's a lot more to the story. You make it sound quick and easy."

"No, it wasn't easy, and it wasn't quick, and I'm sure I have a lot more enemies these days..."

The truck pulled into the familiar drive-in and the past instantly embraced Sally. "You used to take me here when I was a kid. I was always so hungry back then." Sally laughed. "I packed up a lunch this morning, but I felt sorry for the pups and fed them my sandwiches."

"So what you're saying is you're still hungry, just like back then." Adam ordered through the drive-in telephone outside the truck while Sally slowly rubbed the puppy's soft back. "I used to be able to read your mind. Now, I'm not so sure. What are you thinking?" Adam shifted his weight and scooped up the dog.

"I'm thinking about nothing and everything, like I do every day." Sally paused, wondering if she could still confide in her friend, a man she largely ignored during high school because of her changing attitude toward him. "There are for—lack of better words—strange 'feelings' at my house, feelings that are inexplicable on my father's part. He kind of reacts to things...well, very unexpectedly. I know my mother is gone and that might have something to do with it, but… things are…unusual."

"Maybe you just need time to get to know everyone again, including your father."

"I need time to get on with my life. I want to move into a place of my own, but my father responds so adversely to everything. He insists I live at the ranch and work for him, but I have aspirations of my own."

Adam handed the pup and food to Sally. "Maybe your father needs you while he is adjusting to the death of your mother. Why don't you wait it out a while?"

"Because it's not what I want to do. You have been busy while I've been gone. You have a large—extremely large—successful ranch and you hold a district seat... I suppose that's as good as it gets. You've done well."

"Do I detect a note of sarcasm in your tone?"

Sally fed the pup some hamburger meat. "Two seconds ago you told me to sit back and wait for life to come to me. If I would have told you the same thing nine years ago, what would your reaction have been?"

"Touché! You're right, but do stop and take everything into consideration before you make any decisions. Don't get that dog used to table food. You're going to spoil him."

"Have you ever been married?"

Adam smiled. "Have you?"

Sally sat up straight and sighed with frustration. "I wish it were a year from now so we would be talking to each other as friends and not trying to make stupid small talk. So neither of us is or has been married, which of course we both already knew."

"Why did you go off to school anyway? You speak so passionately of ranching. Did you major in agriculture?" Adam ate his food as Sally watched a train slowly begin to move on the tracks.

"No. Actually I was an art major. You should come see my work sometime. I paint windmills mostly—beautiful to look at. They are essential to our existence and yet obtrusive to our landscape." Sally gave another scrap of meat to the puppy. "You know, I really don't know why I lived with my aunt, except that I do remember my father seemed to be very insistent. He raved about the university in New Orleans, and he has always liked my aunt Lucille. It wasn't until my mother's death that my father wrote to me and said it was time to come home even though I resisted the idea at first."

"All sounds pretty normal to me."

Sally smiled. "You always were the pragmatic part of our relationship. I used to hate the fact that you never let me be a hysterical female during my puberty years."

"So, you came home…"

"I attended mom's funeral here in Texas, flew to New Orleans, packed, and flew back. Actually, now that I'm home again, I don't know why I resisted so much. I love it here. Socially, my aunt Lucille was a hoot. I always did have a great time with her, but I can't say that I have accomplished much yet."

"So you're saying a degree is a waste of time?"

"No, I love to paint. It is an extension of who I am and I'm very passionate about what I choose to place on a canvas, but I want to be a landowner. It is hard to explain. Being an artist is not what you do for other people; it is what you do for yourself. It is how you express yourself after you experience life. You can't be an artist if you haven't accomplished or tried to accomplish your dreams, because there is no feeling in the work, no joy."

"It's an interesting perspective. I never quite thought about art in that way."

Sally laughed. "My aunt used to say good art is like pornography; you can't define it but you know it when you see it. She used to read me my mother's letters aloud while I painted. My mother would describe the most beautiful windmills. I would get inspiration from her words as I envisioned the patterns against the sky or the boundaries they formed. I think that's why I paint them. They are a dichotomy of sorts."

"I would love to see your paintings sometime."

"Sure. But to get back to the matters at hand. I want to own my own ranch and run it myself. I want to control my own destiny."

"You plan to do all of this alone?"

Sally was agitated at the lack of empathy. "Do you have a partner running your ranch?"

"Touché, once again."

"You of all people should realize how much I know about ranching just from growing up on the Straight S. I've computerized all the paperwork in my section, and I order all my supplies online. Yesterday, I looked at some fine quarter horses from Ireland on the internet. I can also run any machinery out there in our fields. I know the livestock... What's to stop me from acquiring my own ranch one day?"

"I'm sure nothing. Do whatever you want to. Don't let anything stop you."

"My father used to tell me that about my life."

"Your father is one of the greatest men I know. He has my total admiration."

Sally was surprised. "Why do you say that?"

"Are you kidding? He runs one of the most powerful ranches in the world. Surely you can see the significance of that."

"But he doesn't own it."

"Own the land? It's a matter of power you know, not ownership."

"Well, that's a nice catchy phrase, but I believe in ownership. Ownership is power. I have lived on someone else's ranch for my entire life, and now I have a desire to possess something that is my own and you just said, let nothing get in your way." Sally stuffed five fries in her mouth. Adam had put her on the defensive once again. "All of this wasn't a coincidence, was it?" she finally asked.

"What are you talking about?"

"You being here."

"Being in this truck...being at this drive-in?"

"You know what I mean. Let's face it, you haven't come by to say hello to me in three month's time. The ranches are so close, but you wait until I'm thirty miles away in Benning to ask me out to eat when you were just at the Straight S buying a bull from my father hours ago. I know you must have been out at the ranch on numerous occasions."

"Today you were leaving when I arrived. The rest of the times…well…now just seemed like the right day and time to get acquainted again."

"Why was it up to you?"

"It didn't have to be. You have legs and a mouth."

Sally closed her eyes for a few seconds only to open them in surprise at a loud horn. Instantly, Adam flew out of the truck and slammed the door, agitating the puppy further. It sat up on its haunches and barked, clawing the window with its chubby paws. Sally squinted, her eyes facing the sun as Adam argued with a man she thought she recognized. The yelling lasted only about a minute before Adam flew back into the truck, slammed the door, and started up the engine. He jerked the vehicle in gear but suddenly stopped, screeching the tires. "I'm sorry. Would you mind if we went out to my ranch for a minute?"

Sally didn't answer, her thoughts racing in a thousand different directions.

"Well?" Adam asked impatiently.

"Sure. Why not?" Sally took a deep breath and adjusted herself in the seat as Adam drove out of the parking lot, heading into open country. She sat quietly for a few moments staring at the land ahead. "Adam—"

"Please, don't ask me any questions about what just happened."

"Okay…" Confused by the situation, Sally searched for peace and serenity in the scenery flying by. The wind cooled her sweaty face and nervous disposition. "I know your place is near the Straight S, but where exactly are the boundaries?"

Adam took in a deep breath, gaining his composure. Sally almost gave up on a response, but he finally answered. "Actually, it begins on old Highway 77 about three miles off the main road."

"You mean 'Hobo Highway?' I remember that area as a bunch of chopped up parcels of land. There was always a new trailer house popping up and then being towed away after only a few months. Old man Caste made a fortune selling those tracts and then foreclosing on those poor souls who thought country life was going to be a vacation every day. They didn't realize they had land payments and house payments. Plus they still had to put in a driveway, build a fence. I felt sorry for them. Dad would always complain about the poor animals they left behind. We usually ended up with most of them wandering onto the ranch. It's not divided anymore?"

"No. It's all part of the Hamilton Ranch now. I purchased those segments some years back. You keep saying the ranches are close to each other, but did you know that the Straight S and the Hamilton Ranch actually share a common boundary in that small eastern section in the valley? It's between those lower hills, so it's not an obvious connection."

"No, I didn't. So we are really close neighbors. We're joined at the hip, so to speak." Sally stared out the window, fixing her eyes on the windmills turning tirelessly in the hot sun. "God it's beautiful out here. The serenity of the country doesn't have a price tag, does it? Someday you'll have to tell me how you put together such a large ranch in such a short amount of time."

"Eighteen years is hardly a short amount of time. I was doing this while you were going through junior high and high school and while you were learning to paint windmills."

"But in comparison to generations passing down legacies…"

"If you put it that way, I guess I'd say that I was determined and—"

"Ruthless?"

"Say, where did that come from?"

"Seems like the way of the world these days. People want something, and they go for it any way they can. It's all about money and power."

"Did you learn that in your art classes?"

"I learned that when I grew up. So, can I ask yet what that man wanted? Did I know him?"

"You can ask. It's just business, that's all," Adam said.

"And not mine?"

"Nope."

"Touché back to you! I didn't mean to pry, but I'm here in the truck while you are taking care of your 'business,' and I'm just curious what I'm getting into…"

"You're not getting into anything. I just have to make a phone call and make sure some things are taken care of right away, and then we'll leave."

"Something wrong with your cell?"

"Nope. As a matter of fact, I need to call the ranch to tell them we are coming."

"Okay. Whatever. I guess we need to drop off this cute puppy anyway."

"Yes, before you spoil him rotten."

Adam and Sally passed barbed wire enclosures of green pastures, out buildings, farm machinery, plowed fields still brown, and mesquite-ridden uncleared land. They drove through a metal cattle gate up to an extremely large, old, wooden farmhouse. It had been refurbished but was obviously an original structure of someone's dream from long ago. The second story had white dormer windows while a wraparound porch held chairs and a table with fresh wild flowers in a small cup. There were tall glasses half-filled with clear liquid, droplets of condensation dripping down the outside. Sally noted the items on the table because that was where she was politely instructed to "please wait." Adam took the pup from Sally and passed it on to a ranch hand. She propped her feet up and breathed in the atmosphere of the ranch, the sweet smell of grass dominating the afternoon. Adam's place stretched to the foothills, while windmills jetted up from the horizon along with tall trees and old barns. The scene was unspoiled and simple. Texas was beautiful, and Sally knew at that moment she would have a part of it all to herself one day.

Adam slammed the door as he walked out on the porch. His absence allowed Sally time to absorb the countryside alone. He handed her a soda and pulled a chair out from under the round table with his leg to sit down. "Looks like you've had company recently," she said, pointing to the half-empty glasses.

Adam ignored her remark. He watched Sally stare at the countryside before speaking. "I still have a lot of work to put into this place."

Sally smiled, looking directly into Adam's eyes. "I think it's perfect just the way it is." She turned her attention toward the horizon once again.

"There are experimental grasses to be planted in the fields and…"

But before Adam could continue Sally shot up from her chair and stepped off the porch. "You know today was supposed to be the day that I thought about my future—to put together a plan for me. I was supposed to figure out what I was going to do with the rest of my life. Now here I am with you envying your success and suddenly feeling very sorry for myself. I didn't realize until this moment just how important all of this is to me. I have to own a part of this!" She turned toward him. "I have something important to say, something I just have to tell somebody, and since you were always the one that listened best, I'm going to tell you. It's very personal, and I don't want you to make light of my feelings. I know I mentioned earlier about things being a little weird at home with my dad, but I truly believe that something strange has happened or is happening at the ranch. I'm sure I was sent away from Texas for five years, and I never realized I had been manipulated until my return...until now. I suspected... I have always had a feeling there was something secretive in my father and mother's life, and now I know I am right! Adam," she said desperately, "did you know my mother described this place, your place, from this spot in her letters to me? She wrote so vividly. I've painted those exact windmills."

Sally's alarmed tone increased as she continued.

"How did she know what your ranch looked like? Was she here often?" Sally did not wait or expect an answer. "Was my father here often also? And just why did my father want me to be with you today?"

"Why do you keep asking me that?"

"Please if ever I have asked you to take me seriously in my life... don't disappoint me." She turned toward him. "I remember well in one of my mother's last letters to me. In one part she wrote, 'the sun enjoys sitting on top of the windmills and shining upon all the objects that dared to rise above the horizon, as if to warn them not to try to escape their boundaries.'" She turned away again and looked out over the ranch. "Look at the sun. Look at your windmills, all lined up. Why was this place—your place—haunting my mother? Why did my father want you to be with me today? I've been home for such a long time."

"Stop! Your imagination is running wild. Think about it; technically, you've described a hundred ranches in this area alone that fit your mother's description."

"No, I am an artist. I know what I have painted, and I have painted those windmills."

Adam ignored her remark. "As far as me seeing you, I've been busy…"

Sally sighed. "Unfortunately, you're not really listening. Not this time. An artist can envision the words of a letter." She cried softly.

"Sally, I was over at the Straight S many times toward the end. Your father and I had business. We sat on the porch and had many conversations while your mother lay in her room all day."

"Now I feel jealous about your relationship with my father. That's crappy, isn't it?" Sally wiped her nose with her sleeve.

"I'm trying to say that your mother may not have been very lucid."

"Don't say that about my mother!" Sally's angry reply took Adam by surprise. "It seems you are under the impression that you know more about my family than me. My mother was bright and lucid and she wrote me the most wonderful letters, and they weren't the work of a crazy woman. You want to take her away from me too?"

"I didn't say your mother was crazy. Don't put words in my mouth. I'm just trying to make sense out of something that has you terribly upset. Don't lash out at me. Come back on the porch and sit down."

Sally turned toward the windmills then faced Adam again as she ascended the porch stairs and sat down. "So, for the last time, why did my dad ask you to see me today?"

"What in God's name are you talking about?" Adam towered above Sally, blocking the sun. "Come on. It's time to go back to Benning anyway."

"You're right. It is time." She rose slowly. "I still don't know why you asked me out to begin with."

" Leave it alone! You know you're not in junior high anymore."

A slight breeze suddenly aroused a sense of relief and calmness within Sally, the air enveloping her spirit. "God, Adam, I don't even know why I'm taking my anger out on you. I guess I'm not really upset with you—" Before Sally could finish her sentence, Adam reached for her. He embraced her sunken shoulders and held on. Sally could barely discern the horizon as they stood under the sun, the breeze blowing and the grasses whispering while the windmills creaked and wailed with every turn. It was enough to temporarily heal the anger and confusion. "I needed my confidence back. Thanks." Sally gently pulled free. The two sat on the wooden porch and spoke fondly of the past, visiting about Texas life until the sun began to disappear, a stopwatch for the obtrusive movement and sound of the windmills.

Sally and Adam arrived at the lot in Benning just as the band was setting up to play. Everyone was in good spirits as the day had been a success—not in a monetary sense, but in fellowship. Sally noticed all the Blue Heeler pups were gone and the ponies were grazing on the grass while tied to the lower branches of some of the same trees she had used earlier to shade herself from the hot, Texas sun. Almost everyone knew Adam and greeted him warmly while packing up their wares and paraphernalia. A gentle breeze blew strands of brown hair in her eyes, Sally once again restraining her long mane preparing herself for the evening's festivities.

She helped a few friends pack up their trucks while Adam loaded some unsold square bales of hay back onto a ranch hand's trailer. The noise of the crowd began to escalate as it drew closer to the time the band was supposed to play. Children, dogs, adults, unsold pet rabbits, and horses seemed to move a little faster as the day grew darker. The warm-up notes of the band ushered cheers and hollers from the crowd. Ice chests were hoisted onto the back of the pickups and tailgates were lowered to supply a space for the beer, soda, and people. Pallets were made ahead of time in the back of the trucks for the little ones who would soon grow tired and fall asleep after a busy day. Amazingly enough, when they slept, the noise did not disturb them. The first song was a slow one, and before Sally realized the music had begun she inhabited the middle of the field dancing with Adam. She felt a calmness inside of her, enough to compensate for poor dancing skills and skeptical thoughts.

The night passed all too quickly and Sally felt an incredible sense of belonging with her surroundings. Adam playfully danced with some of the older children who had outlasted the younger ones while she looked on, sitting happily on the back of the pickup drinking a soda provided from an old, red ice chest brought from the ranch. The last song was announced and Adam led Sally to the middle of the field, a passel of children following. They all joined hands and capriciously danced around in a circle giggling, stumbling, and moving to the beat of the music. A herald of claps was heard at the end and, methodically, everyone returned to their pickups, retrieving sleeping children and placing them into the cabs of the trucks. They closed ice chests and secured unsold goods that would probably stay right where they were until the next month's tack sale.

Sally smiled at Adam and admitted honestly, "It was an extraordinary evening. Thanks for your company."

"I had a good time too."

"I suppose I should get in my truck and lead the pack back to the ranch. This time I have to stick with them. My dad will be on the lookout for all of us to be home. It's his family returning."

"The morning comes all too soon, doesn't it? I can think of about a million miles of fence that I need to tend to tomorrow."

"There's always something. With all the spring calves born there never seems to be a time when I don't have one in the holding pen to feed. Hopefully we won't have to deal with summer births."

"Be careful on the way home. Call me when you get back, okay?"

Sally smiled to herself. "Just like the good old days. Listen, about what happened at your ranch earlier, I'm sorry…"

"No need."

"But there is. You were right. I'm not an immature junior high school girl anymore. I should take control of my feelings."

"You're human."

"Forget it, okay? I'm sorry. Leave it at that."

"If that's what you want. Bye."

Adam drove away in his truck as one of the children, Karen, asked Sally if she could ride with her on the way home. Karen, fourteen, often asked Sally's advice about love matters and other problems. She too had called the Straight S home her whole life, her dad being one of many foremen who worked under Sally's father.

"Well, Miss Karen, what is it that you're all smiles about tonight?"

The young girl squirmed uncharacteristically and looked shyly at Sally. "Do you like Mr. Hamilton?" she asked.

"I've known him a long time. He had many, many talks with me years ago like we do now. He was and is very special to me."

"But do you like him, you know, in that way?"

"I know I'll always love him for the security he provided me when I was your age."

"I think you like him now, and I like someone too."

"Really? And who is it? Someone I know?"

"He's a boy who works at the Hamilton Ranch."

"I think I see where this is all leading to. Me thinks I've hatched a plot here."

Karen giggled. "His name is Chris, and he works for Mr. Hamilton; well, his dad does, but I know Chris works there too. They both live on the ranch and take care of one of the cattle sections. He's already seventeen. I can't date yet, but I sometimes see him at the tack sales, and when we make deliveries out to the Hamilton Ranch…"

Sally's senses were aroused. "What do we deliver out to the Hamilton Ranch?"

"I don't know…"

Sally sighed. "Karen!"

"I guess it's stuff like feed, horses, cattle, just ranch stuff. You know…stuff!"

"I wonder why the Straight S would deliver feed to the Hamilton Ranch?" Sally murmured. "I've never even seen any paperwork or heard of anyone going over there."

"Dad's been taking all kinds of stuff over there for about three months now. That's how I met Chris. Duh! Will you take me over to the Hamilton Ranch sometime when you visit?" Karen pleaded, finally revealing her true intent in asking for a ride.

"I don't know when I will be going over there."

"We can go together when we deliver stuff."

"Stuff? You don't have a very extensive vocabulary for a fourteen-year-old." Sally was quiet and pensive on the way home despite Karen's attempts to get a commitment out of her as to when they would indeed go to the Hamilton Ranch and see Chris. She dropped Karen at her house and was able to do some thinking before arriving at her own destination.

Sally felt secure as she softly crept into her own home about midnight. The small house was constructed of wood with a front porch running three quarters around it. An old railing served as an obvious foothold over the years with spur digs in the wood and faded paint around the bottom rung. An old rock fireplace ran the length of one side of the house where the porch stopped. It resembled Adam's house except that it was only one story and on a much smaller scale. Sally thought her father was probably asleep, so she plopped herself down in one of the easy chairs facing the fireplace. Memories raced through her mind, and tears filled her eyes as she thought of those rare moments when her mother read stories to her in the winter in front of a roaring fire. She learned how to sew in this room and play the piano and… A knock interrupted her thoughts as she peered intently toward the window and saw a figure standing by the door.

"Who is it?" she asked quietly, not wanting to disturb her father.

"It's Adam. Can I talk to you for a minute?"

Sally opened the door as it creaked in protest.

"There's a breeze out," Adam said. "Why don't we talk on the porch?"

The need to be out in the open was good. Sally gladly joined him. "Is there something wrong?" she whispered.

"No. I felt guilty about not seeing you home."

Sally laughed. "What a strange thing to say. I had an entourage of about fifty people."

"Nevertheless, I should have followed you home."

"You're not my keeper anymore. I officially relieve you of the responsibility, but it was a terribly nice and considerate thought. Thanks. I'm kinda wound up, anyway. I would like someone to talk to." Facing Adam, she asked him if he wanted something to drink, but before he could answer, Sally confronted him about the deliveries to his ranch. "What does the Straight S deliver to the Hamilton Ranch?" she asked quite suddenly.

"Deliveries? What deliveries?"

"Karen Hollister told me tonight that she had a crush on this boy, Chris, whose dad works for you at your ranch. The way she met him was when she went with her father to deliver 'stuff', as she so eloquently describes everything, to the Hamilton Ranch. I was just wondering what we deliver from here to you that you couldn't get… well, you know, at a feed store. I was also wondering why I never knew anything about it."

"Karen Hollister has a crush on Chris?" Adam asked.

"Please don't evade the question."

"And the question, this time, was…"

"You know what I'm asking!"

Sally's dad walked out of the house, smoking a pipe. "I thought I heard voices out here." He turned toward Sally. "Everybody get back okay tonight, honey?" he asked seriously.

"Sure, Dad. Everything went fine. Everyone had a great time as usual."

"That's good. Glad to hear it. They all deserve a break once a month. And they all try to peddle that junk they make around here, too." He shook Adam's hand. "Hi, son. Glad to see that bull didn't get the better of you this morning. I see you're still in one piece." Mr. McKenna sat down in one of the chairs, propped his feet up, and puffed on his pipe. His silver hair and mustache shone in the moonlight and his dark, wrinkled face moved slightly and methodically as he peered about the ranch that stretched out in front of him.

Adam and Sally exchanged glances.

"I know what you're thinking," the older man said, "I wasn't invited to this party, was I? I hope ya'll don't mind the intrusion."

"No, of course not," Sally said right away. "In fact, I was just asking Adam about the supplies we deliver to the Hamilton Ranch on a regular basis."

"We don't send any supplies to his ranch on a regular basis." Mr. McKenna stayed in his same position and never turned toward his daughter. He blew rings of smoke slowly around his pipe.

"One of the kids on the ranch, you know her, Karen Hollister, said she goes with her dad to deliver—"

"She probably goes with her dad to visit some friends. A lot of the workers on Hamilton Ranch came from here. They're all still friends. Hell, they're family, and probably exchanging canned goods, and all that junk they make during the year." He turned slowly toward Sally. "Don't you think?" he asked seriously.

Sally shifted uneasily. "Sure, Dad, whatever you say."

"Well, guess it's bedtime for me. Don't stay up too late. Good night, Adam." He shook Adam's hand and went back into the house.

Sally spun toward Adam and pleaded, "What the hell is going on around here?"

Adam smiled. "Calm down. What are you talking about?"

"I am so sick of hearing that same exact question from you and my father. All of you act like I'm mentally incapable of a thought. I am talking about the fact that every time I bring up a question there seems to be a convenient explanation to everything I ask."

"Maybe because there is."

"And maybe because there is not." Sally faced the open field and remained silent for a while. "You can see the lights of your house from here. How strange. Your place seems so close. Yet I know we're miles away."

"I told you earlier that some small sections of my land adjoin the Straight S."

"Yes, I suppose so," Sally said, slowly and pensively.

Adam physically forced Sally to face him as if trying to break some kind of spell. "You know, you are like my place right now—so close, and yet so far away." Adam kissed her on the forehead.

"Adam, you came back into my life today after a long absence and, like a bright diversion, you temporarily distracted me from reality, but the irony is you have complicated my life even more. There is something awfully wrong here. And you know what it is. I feel it. My father is so distant—not that he hasn't always been quiet and serious—but some of his strength has turned to bitterness or something that I cannot explain. I've waited three months to finally say aloud to someone who I know well that I am *not* the problem here at home. I returned to a problem. I desperately need to find out some answers to some questions. The trouble is, I don't know the questions to ask."

Adam sighed at his momentary loss for words. "I don't know how I can explain something you feel I am a part of. Anyway, I wish you luck in your endeavor." The sadness in Adam's voice matched Sally's pensive state. He walked away, leaving her standing on the porch staring deep into a lost horizon. As the moon escaped some sparse clouds, silhouetted windmills suddenly appeared before Sally.

"Oh my God," she said. "Are they warning me not to escape my boundaries like they did my mother?"

CHAPTER TWO

Windmills have their secrets.
Don't tell me it ain't so.
Why jet above the landscape
And not tell us what you know?

You stand so strong unyielding
For those below your gears.
Some sit and lie against you,
Calming summer fears

You speak all day to those who hear,
So many in the field.
Your language is a special gift.
How many have you healed?

Sally awoke the next morning to an obtrusive sounding alarm clock. She groaned and trudged into the kitchen to retrieve a cup of coffee. One of the things she insisted on when she returned home was the acquisition of a coffee pot that had the coffee ready when you walked into the kitchen. Her dad followed close behind, as they both always awoke at 5:00 a.m.

"Why don't you sleep in this morning? You were up late last night." Mr. McKenna shuffled outside on the porch to drink his first cup of coffee, the same routine every morning, come hurricanes or tornadoes. Today, Sally followed him out.

"Dad, about last night. I need to talk to you."

Not seeming to hear his daughter, he gazed out toward the horizon and commented mostly to the land in front of him. "Don't think I could start the day without looking out and seeing what lies ahead of me."

"Dad, I want to talk to you," Sally said, frustrated. She remembered all too well the distance between them growing up. Nothing had changed.

"You wanna talk about supplies to the Hamilton Ranch?"

"No." Sally paused. "I want to know why you insisted I go live with Aunt Lucille in New Orleans."

"A ranch out in the middle of nowhere was no place for a young person. You had to go to college and your mother and I talked it over and thought it would be the best place for you. You had a relative there."

"But there were colleges closer than—"

"What does it matter? If we had sent you to one here in Texas, would you question now why you didn't go out of state?"

"No. I don't think I would actually. Every time I try to talk to you, Daddy, you get upset with me."

"No, honey. I…look, maybe you should have gone to one of the Texas universities. I don't know. It's easy to look back—"

"Daddy, that's not really the point. The truth is things just don't seem right here. When I was in New Orleans, it was like you didn't want me home as long as Mom was alive."

"I've got work to do." Sally's sadness swelled as she traced her dad's walk into the house. The Straight S was not the home she once knew.

About 10:00 a.m. Sally passed on her duties to one of the other workers. She drove toward a locally owned real estate office located just outside the small town that supplied everyone a common ground for gossip in the area. Lying in bed the night before, she definitely decided to buy a small parcel of land and live on her own outside the Straight S. A close friend of her mother's held a partnership with another woman from the area and, because Sally had called earlier, she knew the office would be expecting her. The two women started the business after their husbands died. For income, they sold portions of their ranches after dividing them into small tracts, supplying each one with electricity and water. One thing led to another and soon they sold farms, larger tracts, commercial property, and a few residential homes that had survived in the small town. Actually, Sally thought, her visit was twofold. Mrs. Wright had been a good friend of her mother's, so she might possibly acquire more than land if she played her cards right. The older woman greeted her warmly and they sat on the couch in the small lobby area drinking coffee.

"You're looking so good." She smiled as she patted Sally's leg.

"Thanks, Mrs. Wright. You are too."

"Now, what's this about you wanting some land? And you living on that huge ranch…"

"I just want a few acres to begin with. I thought I'd bring my horses over from the Straight S and run a few cattle. Between you and me, the cattle would be to get my agricultural exemption, of course, while I put in some orchards this winter and build a training pen for horses. I couldn't pay the taxes otherwise, not until I start getting an income from the land. I guess maybe about forty acres to begin with would be good. Ideally, I'd like something with more acreage adjoining so I could have the option to buy more when I could afford it."

"You still gonna be workin' at the Straight S?"

"For a while…"

The woman peered at Sally above her reading glasses. "I see." She stepped over to her desk and retrieved a thick, commercial book and a few papers. "Well, I could show you some land and get with you this afternoon after I do some calling and digging."

"I suppose we'll have to talk about price this afternoon too," Sally said, with some reservation.

"Let's see what we can find."

"You have a few minutes to talk, Mrs. Wright?"

"You wanna talk about your mama, don't you?" She didn't wait for Sally to answer. "I'll tell you what—I do have an appointment in a while and I have some homework to do first, but anything you want to know, let's discuss while I take you to look at some land you're gonna buy from me!"

"Sure… Mrs. Wright, have you sold any land to Adam Hamilton?"

The bell on the door jingled but neither Mrs. Wright nor Sally paid attention to the sound. "Adam Hamilton is one of my best customers."

"Thank you. It's nice to be known as the best." Both Sally and Mrs. Wright looked up. "What's going on here? Am I being discussed without an opportunity to defend myself?"

Mrs. Wright was a lighthearted woman. "I think I'll get back to my computer. See you this afternoon, Sally." She looked at Adam. "Did you need something, hon?"

"No. I can see you're busy. It can wait."

Sally walked quickly out of the door, Adam following with equal resonance. She stopped and turned toward him, a little embarrassed.

"Were you inquiring about me in there?" Adam asked, with a mixture of confusion and anger in his voice.

"I just wanted to know if you had bought land from Mrs. Wright, that's all."

"Why?"

"I don't know. We were just talking. That's all."

"Have I done something to you to make you distrust me?"

"No, I was just curious about who you bought your land from."

"Why?"

"I don't know. I have to go." Sally quickly jumped into her truck. "Sorry if I offended you."

Adam leaned up against the window. "You don't trust me. What reason—"

"I'm just trying to unravel the mysteries surrounding my life. I don't know what I expected to hear. Talking with Karen last night made me think—"

"Sally, she's fourteen years old."

"I'm sorry. It really is none of my business."

"How about you come out to my place around noon for lunch today?" Adam asked unexpectedly.

"Okay. Sure." Sally watched Adam drive away. *I'll have just enough time to get some letters from home.*

Sally returned to the Straight S just in time to see her father gallop-ing up to the house and securing a protesting horse to the railing of the porch. He stomped up the steps and slammed the door while yanking off his dusty hat and hitting it against his leg. Sally sat in the truck, wondering if her desertion for the morning been discov-ered and contemplated if retaliation was at hand. Sally sighed to herself. "There was one way to find out," she thought aloud.

"Hi, Dad! I'm home!" she yelled as she tossed her purse on the chair and walked into the kitchen. John turned and glared at Sally while setting the cold water jug from the refrigerator down hard on the table, splashing some of its contents.

"Where the hell have you been?" he shouted. "I phoned you from the truck on your cell and got no answer. Just had the vet out. That heifer had her calf early. I don't think it's gonna make it! Get a bottle and get out to the barn in the west field. Bring some warm water and a couple of gallons of that skim milk. Hell, bring that concoc-tion you make up, the one you use on the other newborns. That calf needs your special touch. He should have already had it."

Sally surmised that the calf must be important if her dad was so angry. She did have a special touch with the animals and had saved many a calf, duckling, bunny, foal, and chick from ultimate demise. There was always an experiment of some kind going on in breeding, crossbreeding, and generally trying to improve the herds. This must be one of her father's own babies. He had often been written up in the *Texas Stockman* for his accomplishments in successful breeding and grafting of certain grasses that Texas cattle could thrive on for less money than in the past. But this would mean that her meeting with Mrs. Wright would have to be postponed for another day.

Sally arrived at the west barn in split-second time, just after her conversation with Mrs. Wright canceling her appointment. The small calf lay in the straw, breathing heavily on its side, eyes wide open, begging for help. All the hands ceremoniously moved to the side as Sally walked in. She cried to herself. She could never get used to the helplessness of some of the animals she came across on the Straight S. Nature was cruel sometimes and it was her job to thwart nature's wrath if possible. Sally's dad did not follow her because he knew there was nothing he could do. His daughter was experienced and knowledgeable and needed a free hand to follow her own instincts. Anyone present at this point would be useless and possibly detrimental. The vet had delivered the calf; his job was finished.

"Hello, little fellow. It's all right. I'm here to help you." Sally stroked the calf and after laying all her "tools" close at hand and slowly lifted him, manipulating his head in her lap carefully. She breathed close to the little animal's face and rubbed her cheek against his still wet head. He was just hours old. She hoped nature had not already convinced the little animal to let go. The echo of a sad wail could be heard as Sally thought of the mother and her beckoning to the lost calf that disappeared so soon after birth. Although the mother longed for her calf, she was weak and useless to the baby now. Cows are so touched by their calves it is ironic when their babies are taken away every year; the wailing continues for sometimes two or three nights on the ranch. Those were among the saddest moments Sally experienced. She began her long and dubious task.

Sally whispered to the calf, caressing him around his warm, wet nose and dry mouth. She blew her warm breath on his face, between his eyes and around his mouth. After she had stroked him, whispered to him, and allowed her scent to constantly be exposed to him, she slipped the bottle between his teeth and squeezed as she rubbed her hand up and down his wet, furry throat to prevent him from choking. She also raised him up and down slightly, causing constant but sparse movement throughout his frail, limp body. She repeated soft, kind words over and over as she bent down in-between squirts to allow the calf to breathe in her essence. There wasn't a spot on the young calf's hide she didn't stroke. Sally methodically rubbed the bottle all around the calf's mouth as she whispered to and petted the animal.

Sally finally relaxed and lay back, eyes closed, as the calf breathed easier and had at last taken some nourishment in his swollen stomach. *If only he'll keep eating,* Sally thought, painfully sore from constantly bending over her helpless patient. She knew the injections the vet gave him would help fight pneumonia, a common cause of death because of the inactivity of the premature animal. She would continue the injections for months if the calf lived that long.

Her back ached, and her neck felt as though it wasn't a part of her body. She glanced at the door of the barn, the sun settling on the horizon, the windmills absent from the scene. Smiling, she eased him up again and rubbed the calf's wet head, his languid tongue searching for more milk. He'd already taken two bottles from Sally. *A good sign*, she thought but knew that the weeks ahead of hand-feeding this little fellow every four hours, day in and day out, would guarantee little survival. It was impossible to determine at this point whether he was fully developed at birth. She shut her eyes again, feeling it would soon be safe to transport the calf closer to home in a pen outside her house. While Sally was resting, calf asleep in her lap, she suddenly remembered the lunch date with Adam. But as though he had sensed her thoughts, Adam appeared in the barn and headed straight toward the calf. He stretched his large hand over his rapidly pulsating heart to feel the strong beat. He then crouched and placed his ear on his chest to check if the calf's lungs were clear. Smiling, he perched next to Sally, still peering at the calf. "You do good work."

"You know as well as I do, my work has only just begun."

"Take good care of him. He's mine, you know."

"Really? Is he the result of a cross-breeding experiment?" Sally asked with enthusiasm.

"You're looking at ten long, tedious years of research. Your dad and I have been working on this project together."

"He never told me. Neither did you."

"Should I have?" Adam stroked the calf affectionately.

"Is it some secret?"

"Do we spar next?"

Sally fell back on some hay, moving the calf slightly under his protests. "I'm too exhausted to spar. As a matter of fact, I was just about to call for a truck and some help to get this guy back to the house." Sally stretched. "You know, I did ask if you did business with the Straight S."

"He is definitely not business. He is my passion."

"What's so special about him?" Sally asked as she stared into the calf's round, watery brown eyes.

"He's supposed to be the sturdiest of the sturdy," Adam said confidently. "He'll survive on little grass like his Longhorn brother, but he'll be meatier and stouter." Adam instinctively nestled next to Sally, reaching for her tired hand while she stroked the sleeping calf affectionately. "Your dad called and said he was born early. I figured that's why you didn't show up. John convinced me not to come over here right away. He said you needed time to perform your magic."

"Do you think birthing is going to be a problem among this breed?"

"Possibly, if this little fellow is any indication. That's one of the kinks we'll have to figure out. Indulge me and don't take him back yet. Let him lie in your lap for a while longer. He looks very comfortable."

Sally stroked the calf, relishing that history was being made right in front of her eyes. What an awesome thought, to create something which would benefit all mankind. Sally and Adam relaxed in the barn together. *This could be mine,* she thought sadly, *the pink and blue sky beaming its light through the barn door and windows, God's spotlight on the new baby.* As the sun set, Adam tenderly squeezed Sally, and she allowed the earlier serenity to replace her frustration.

Adam sighed. "It's sundown, and I'm being selfish. You've been tending to the calf all day. You must be exhausted."

"Actually, the events of the day have rejuvenated my mind and body." Sally leaned forward. "Let me rub his chest and move him around a bit to make sure fluid hasn't settled in his lungs."

Adam watched Sally work with the calf and admired her instincts and knowledge as she repeated her earlier meticulous movements. A good instinct was half the battle in ranching and farming. At that moment he realized there was so much he wished he could tell her. "Come on, we'll transport him back in my truck. I'll lift him." Adam languidly arose and Sally winced as she stood up, her stiff body aching with every movement. She felt dirty and sticky but satisfied and peaceful. *The calf could hardly have survived,* she thought, *if he wasn't a sturdy breed as Adam described. What a price this bull will bring once he's old enough, and what a herd he will produce for future generations.*

As Adam placed his hands on Sally's shoulders and began rubbing her neck, Mr. McKenna stomped into the barn, spouting questions as fast as his intrusion. Adam smiled as he stepped away from Sally, and, without incident, the calf was transported to a small, covered corral located next to the porch of the house.

Three vehicles sat in a row in front of the McKenna house, the pink sky settling on each one simultaneously. The former occupants of the trucks were all sitting on the porch drinking coffee.

John's eyes searched the ranch—that familiar, distant stare Sally observed so often since arriving home, that same stare she observed as a child. Adam broke the silence with a yell.

"Yes! By God, we did it, John! And he's just the beginning."

"That calf has a ways to go yet. In the beginning the vet techs will be in the pen twenty-four/seven except when Sally is feeding him. She's really the key in whether he'll make it or not."

Adam turned toward Sally. "I have confidence in your daughter to get him through this questionable time."

"Yes," commented John, "she's a wonderful girl."

Sally stretched and smiled. "It's not nice to tease Florence Nightingale. I need to shower and wash my hair, or I may die myself. If you'll excuse me, I'll be back in about twenty minutes." Sally entered the living room to a ringing phone. To her delight, it was Mrs. Wright.

Sally plopped down, phone in hand. "Hi, Mrs. Wright. I'm glad you called. In fact, you just caught me coming into the house."

"Listen, sweetie, I have some listings here you may be interested in. In fact"—Sally heard some papers rustling in the background—"I'll be here until 9:00, if you want to drop by the office."

Sally hadn't been able to think about her land all day, but now, with renewed excitement, her energy level suddenly rose. "I've been nursing a newborn calf all day, but I'll jump in the shower and be there as soon as I can. I'm kind of on a time schedule now with this new four-legged baby in the picture, but I don't have to feed him again until 10:00 this evening, and if there's an emergency the vet tech is with him and I believe two very willing sitters!"

"That sure brings back fond memories. But I wouldn't do it again in this lifetime!" Mrs. Wright said, somewhat seriously.

"But this one is different," Sally said with pride in her voice. She hung up the phone and quickly showered changing into a cool, cotton dress. After being in jeans all day it felt good to have something loose on her body. She pushed open the creaking porch door.

"That's some change," Adam commented, the fading sun and light from the house providing strategically placed shadows.

Sally's wet hair hung loosely around her shoulders and down her back. She searched the porch. "Did Dad go inside already?"

"Yes, he said he was going to bed at a decent hour tonight."

"I've got an appointment with Mrs. Wright."

"I heard. I listened in on your telephone conversation. Actually, your dad and I both heard."

"So, did he want you to talk me out of going?"

"Something like that." Adam's propped-up foot slammed down suddenly, and he placed his coffee cup on the table. "You haven't eaten anything all day."

Sally hadn't forgotten. "I'll tend to that when I get home. Mrs. Wright will only be at the office until 9:00."

"I'll take you."

"Are you offering me a ride or doing my dad a favor?"

"I do owe you a meal. The vet tech is with the calf. How about a bite after we meet with Mrs. Wright? We'll have time before 10:00 rolls around. Does your neck still hurt?" Adam placed his hands on her almost bare brown shoulders. Sally felt extremely peaceful, but peace has a way of withdrawing itself as the world closes in and—in this case—young Karen Hollister riding up on her horse to deliver a message to Adam.

"You two seem to be awful cozy looking," she teased, as she walked up to the porch and handed a piece of paper to Adam. Sally reached down and sipped cold coffee, observing Adam's facial expression as he read the note.

"Thanks, Karen," he finally said, with a look of consternation. "Tell your dad I'll take care of the situation."

Karen smiled and tried to wink at Sally as she walked away.

"Don't forget to rub down that horse!" Sally yelled, as the young girl mounted the spotted mare and rode off.

"What did the note say?"

"Just something about some cattle."

"What cattle?"

"Nothing. It's ranch business."

"And not mine, I suppose? I am part of this ranch, you know."

"But not mine."

"Technically, that girl's father works for me, so if this has to do with Straight S cattle…"

"It doesn't. Make up your mind. You don't want to be a part of this ranch anyway. Why does it make such a big difference to you?"

"I'm here now. Just because I've got greater aspirations than working for someone else all my life…" Sally turned toward the horizon. "You did, too. Do I have to remind you of what you've been up to the last eighteen years?"

"My father didn't need me like your father needs you."

"Oh, be serious."

"I thought I was."

"There's a hundred out-of-work ranch hands qualified to fill my shoes. What I do is an everyday, newspaper-hiring job and you know it."

"I don't know of anyone who could have done what you did today— and do *not* attempt to minimize your role in saving that calf's life."

Sally paused and stared at Adam. "Won't you please support me in this?" She gently squeezed his arm. Her touch stirred fond memories.

"I don't know if there is anything mysterious to support."

"Then I'll have to prove it to you."

"My business and the Hamilton Ranch is strictly my own and has absolutely nothing to do with your dad. I want you to know that from the start."

"Those words are cryptic." Suddenly, Sally felt a chill.

"Are you listening to me?"

"Sure. We'd better go if we're going to make it in time to Mrs. Wright's office.

"Let's take my truck," Adam said as he grabbed her hand, "since we are going out to dinner afterward. Let's check on the calf and make sure he doesn't need you until his next feeding. I want to make sure the vet tech has both yours and my cell phone number."

Sally and Adam drove up to the small real estate office, a light visible through one of the windows. A curtain was pulled to the side and then released after they had knocked.

"Hi," Mrs. Wright said as she smiled and pulled on the stubborn door. "Oh, hello, Adam." She hesitated. "Ya'll come in. Excuse the locked door, but when I'm here by myself, there's no tellin' what might happen. You know one can't be too careful, especially a widow alone, even an old one like me. Here, Adam, sit down. Get that chair, will ya, hon?"

Mrs. Wright spoke incessantly the minute the two stepped in. The older lady snuggled behind her desk in a large chair and rolled her way up to some scattered papers. "Now I've got a rather long list here of land that's for sale." She peered up and smiled. "I really didn't know you would be here, Adam."

Sally studied the gaze between them. "It's okay. He's here to help."

"Sure, honey," she said, breaking the fixed look between Adam and herself. "First of all, there's thirty acres on old farm road twenty…"

Sally listened intently as Mrs. Wright explained the computer printout. The largest parcel of land for sale was fifty acres, the smallest five.

"You can keep this printout. I have everything on record. Got it from my husband. He was a stickler for records. Spent hours on the computer, even back in the day when everyone and their mother didn't own one yet. He had all his ranch business and other matters on the computer—his whole life is behind this screen." She stroked the machine with affection. "But, this appointment book here." She slapped the pages. "My schedule stays on paper. Some things you just can't mess with." She thumbed through her paper calendar. "I'm free the day after tomorrow…"

"That's fine, Mrs. Wright, but I'm on a bit of a schedule with this new calf. Do you have anything around 11:00? That will give me time to feed my newly acquired baby. I'm free then until 2:00."

Sally watched Adam pick up the computer printout from the desk and study it intently as he walked around the room. She arranged a meeting time with Mrs. Wright and then both she and Adam were out the door and in the truck headed for a small café located on the highway next to the Straight S.

Adam stared at the printout as they waited for their food. "See anything on that list you may be interested in?"

"Possibly," he said quietly. "Personally, I'm hungrier than anything else, and you've only got about forty-five minutes left before the calf will need feeding again."

"He's got someone with him. He's not alone."

"But the calf needs you for feeding, your gut instinct and common sense. He's too important to me and your father, of course."

"You don't have to remind me. That calf is on the Straight S, not on the Hamilton Ranch."

Adam sighed heavily. "So I need to beg you to do your job?"

"I'll do my job and I'll do it well. I guess we're really getting to know each other again. We are fighting over everything."

"I'm sorry. I take what I do very seriously."

"And I don't because I have an agenda of my own?"

"Your first responsibility is to the Straight S."

"Who says? I'm here because my father asked me to be here. You sound like my life revolves and depends on someone else's ranch—very cryptic."

"Not that nonsense again."

"You're right. It's all nonsense. You think everything I feel is all in my imagination, well I intend to build a life that does not include the Straight S."

"Are you sure?"

"Yes, I'm sure."

"Right… Getting back to the calf; it took me eighteen years to get where I am today and ten of those years went into that calf lying in that holding pen outside of your house. I really don't want to give up ten years because—"

"Because of me? Do you not respect or trust me at all? Is total disdain your whole image of me?"

"I didn't mean to imply irresponsibility, but I didn't get to this point in my life by being subservient to whims."

Sally thought the conversation could not get any worse. Ironically, the Straight S sounded like a pretty good alternative place to be right now. *Havens are often unexpected dwellings,* she thought. Both ate quietly.

As the pair pulled up to the house, Sally practically leaped from the truck and headed straight to the holding pen as she tucked the computer paper carelessly into her leather purse alongside the letters from her mother, flinging the handbag recklessly on the gate post. Because Adam was with her, Sally was not able to show the letters from her mother to Mrs. Wright. Sally discovered the calf sleeping peacefully, but he began bawling, opening his soulful eyes to a familiar sight. The vet tech left, and, to Sally's delight, the calf struggled up on all fours, something calves usually do right away. She hugged and stroked him affectionately, placing her face against his cold, wet nose. "You've been practicing while I've been gone. No wonder you were asleep. I'll bet you're hungry." Sally exited the pen and locked it carefully before heading toward the house to prepare a special feed for the calf. She combined a concoction of milk, soy proteins, and baby cereal in a metal bucket along with two bottles she had already filled in preparation for a ravishing, impatient baby animal.

Sally unlocked the gate carefully as she was precariously balancing bottles and buckets at the same time. She glanced up to see the calf rubbing against Adam as he was diligently examining the small animal's eyes, ears, and legs. The vision before her touched Sally's heart. Power and compassion were an unusual combination. "I promise I'm not going to neglect him," she said, struggling with the paraphernalia.

"I didn't think you would. Please understand. This calf represents a large part of the struggle in my life. It is, for lack of a better word, my creation."

"I'll feed him when you're finished."

"I'll never be finished."

"You know what I mean. I need room to work."

Adam stopped stroking the fragile beast. "After this calf there will be another, and then another. There will always be a section of raw land with experimental grasses, or a new breed just around the corner, or irrigation improvements." Getting no reaction from Sally, Adam began a tirade of words. "I have battled hurricanes from the coast, tornadoes from the belt, too much rain, too little rain, parasites from the ground, and people who think they know better than those who have already fought the battles. And look at what is before you—a helpless creature that may change the way we ranch, eat, live, or it may simply die in the next minute—its existence known only to a few. This land has not made me into a pacifist or a coward. You have to know what you are capable of doing and what is impossible to tackle."

"We all have our battles. Some may not be as blatant or obvious as yours."

"You don't see it. It's the same battle for everyone." He turned from Sally, resuming his examination of the calf and spoke as though going against his better judgement. "I don't think there is any great mystery surrounding your life worth stirring up trouble over. Asking questions may hurt people's lives."

"Are you talking about my father?"

"He's a good man. People make decisions in their lives all the time, and they do it because they think it is the right thing to do at the time."

"Do you know something about my father you think I should hear?"

"That's impossible to know at this point, but I'll help you if I can."

Sally stared past Adam and then extended her hand. "Partners?"

Adam smiled and squeezed Sally's hand. "I thought we already were."

The calf began bawling, and Sally snuggled comfortably in the hay, repeating the earlier day's ritual with the same loving hands and heart. She gazed up periodically at Adam. Everything he'd said about Texas was true. Ranching was a tough life; there were never any guarantees. Many people lost their souls and all their possessions in just one or two bad seasons. Perhaps this was why her father didn't ever acquire his own land. Maybe he couldn't handle the risk.

Adam watched Sally intently as she fed the calf. She knew when to insert the bottle into the calf's mouth and when to remove it. Her nurturing spurred the animal to suckle the bottle. The little fellow responded eagerly and begged for more food, but overfeeding it would be just as bad as no food at all, so Sally wisely quit and gently hugged him instead. Again, she repeated her ritual with the calf as he responded with heavy, wet sighs. Sally injected him with some additional medicine from the vet, and Al—as she had affectionately named him—laid his head in her lap and fell asleep. Her soul stirred, and her heart cried, knowing how helpless and dependent he was.

What irony, she thought. *There was always the chance one or both of us might not survive.*

Adam urged Sally to stand and affectionately assisted her in collecting the bottles and buckets. "I'll wash them at the next feeding," she commented, feeling as though the life was suddenly drained from her. Sally stood on the porch, her collection in hand. She paused and turned toward Adam.

"Go to bed and get some rest."

"Are you still fired up?" Sally asked, smiling.

"Naw," he said and climbed into the truck and drove away.

CHAPTER THREE

Windmills line the boundaries,
Guarding soil that man will sow.
They join with fence, together
Protecting fields that grow.

An endless job with no relief
Fences a farmer mends,
But windmills stand against the sky.
Their vision never ends.

The scheduled alarms for the feedings seemed to come more and more often as Sally felt compelled to stay with Al to nurture his spirit. She caught bits of sleep in the afternoon, making it a little easier to respond to her rigorous schedule, but just keeping the books—even on the computer—for only a minor section of the ranch seemed endless, much less the handling of the worker's problems, feeding Al, and trying to attend to her father's needs. There was no time to practice her barrel racing, no time to paint, no time to discover the mysteries that surrounded her life. At 10:00 p.m. the next evening, Sally was preparing food for the little calf when she heard a truck drive up. The front porch door creaked opened and slammed shut. "Dad? Is that you?" Suddenly a chill overcame her as she turned to see Bill Tans standing in the kitchen doorway. "Hello,

Mr. Tans. Can I help you?" she asked weakly, her voice trembling. Bill Tans was Adam's assistant foreman. He used to work on the Straight S at one time.

"I was looking for your dad."

"Is something wrong at the Hamilton Ranch that I could help—"

"No. I'll wait here on the couch for your dad to return."

"I'd rather you wait on the porch." Sally shifted Al's bottles nervously in her arms.

Bill smiled before he reluctantly pushed open the screen door to the porch. He stumbled out and slumped on a chair next to the table.

Sally wished her dad would return because feeding Al at this moment was not an option. She set Al's bottles down and nervously tried her father on his cell. The front door opened once again. "Dad?" she asked, with hope in her voice.

"Now that's the second time you've called me dad." I was just thinking out there that you hadn't asked me if I wanted something to drink."

"We don't have any alcohol in the house."

"You trying to tell me that old man of yours don't drink? That's a good one."

"You've obviously had enough."

"You've got a mouth on you, just like your daddy. But I can shut him up real quick with what I know. Now you may be a different story." He inched closer to Sally. She hit the back of her legs on the table as she backed away from the horrible man's scent.

"I ain't going to hurt you."

"Then get the hell out of my house, now!"

Tans laughed, paused, and then half stomped, half stumbled out the door. "That's okay, girlie. I've got some bottles in the truck."

Sally tried her father on the cell again, but Adam answered. "Come to my house, now. Please hurry…" Sally's voice trailed as tears filled her eyes and she nervously dropped the phone.

A few minutes passed before Sally heard the gravel and dirt protesting beneath truck tires. Threatening voices on the porch followed, music to her ears.

"Why the hell are you here, man? I thought we settled all of this again the other day!" Adam shouted, clearing the table of booze bottles with a sweep of his hand.

"I've worked my hours at your ranch, Hamilton. I have business with John. It's not your business." Tans stumbled and fell forward on the porch rail.

"You're a worthless drunk, Bill. Go home! I'll handle this with John."

"You? That's a laugh. You're tighter than hell with McKenna as it is now. That new visitor in town...that's trouble right there. And now you and his daughter—"

"Shut up or I'll shut you up!"

"When am I going to get what's coming to me?"

"What the hell do you think you deserve? You were doing your lousy job, Bill, and you got paid for it like everyone else."

"Who are you trying to fool?"

John's truck raced up the gravel driveway, stopping inches from the house. Knowing Adam was already there was a small comfort as his eyes were drawn toward the intruder in his house. Adam's immediate departure in the only available truck delayed John's defense of his own home and daughter. He immediately confronted the drunk man, grabbing him by his filthy shirt, ignoring Adam's presence for the moment. "Get the hell off my land, Tans, before I throw you off."

"This ain't your land, remember?" He stared at both Adam and John before pulling away. There was an eerie silence, and then he backed off.

Adam yanked the door open beckoning Sally's name. "Sally? Sally, where are you? Are you okay?"

"No." Sally loosened the grip on the butcher knife, daring to breathe normally at last. She glared at Adam and her father, who had followed him into the kitchen. "What the hell was that all about?"

Adam and John McKenna stared at each other silently. Sally waited, glaring first at Adam and then at her father, fully intending to get an answer but to no avail. "That's just great. I'm scared half to death and I'm not even going to know why. Do you both think I'm stupid?" She slammed the knife on the counter. "I feel like such a fool. Which one of you is going to try to convince me now that there's nothing going on around here? You both make me sick." Sally wiped the tears from her chin. "I've got to feed Al. If you both will excuse me, I've got work to do, as I have been so graciously reminded many times over." Sally gathered her buckets and bottles and stormed from the house. She entered Al's holding pen crying. Sally set her bottles down immediately while petting the calf affectionately as he rubbed up against her leg. He was loud and noisy and still very wobbly, but was progressing as well as could be expected at this time. Al tried sucking on Sally's fingers while she was nervously filling the bottles, spilling much of the special formula. She finally settled him down with her usual ritual and gently eased the bottle into his mouth. Al obviously felt her anxiety, but instinctively drank and then laid his head down in her lap, a habit he seemed to be getting accustomed to. "You trust me, don't you?" Sally lay back and relaxed, the dependent calf already asleep. She sweetly stroked his dry hide. "I've got to go," she finally whispered. Al did not hear her.

Sally loudly rinsed out the bottles and bucket in the kitchen sink. "Let's go for a ride."

"Well, Adam, did you and my father have a pleasant conversation?"

"What I have to say will only take a few minutes. I know you need to sleep."

Sally wiped her hands on a red checkered kitchen towel and tossed it on the counter as she turned. "I'll get some straight answers?"

"Yes."

"Then I'll go for a ride." Sally opened the refrigerator and snatched a Coke. "Want one?"

"No, thanks." Sally sighed and ceremoniously followed Adam out the door and into the darkness. She passed a sleeping calf and smiled as she hopped into the vehicle. Al was still being cared for by the vet tech. She noticed he had just given Al an injection while he was sleeping.

Adam expertly maneuvered his truck through the summer Texas night. The moon was full, lighting the bumpy county road. They passed field after field, fence upon fence. They drove through rolling hills toward a jagged horizon, its smooth line broken up by the ever-present, ever-mindful windmills; they passed barns, standing animals, fallen down sheds, stock ponds, and farm machinery. The country again supplied Sally the necessary contentment to weather the latest storm. She laid her head back and breathed in the night's sweet blend of cooling grass and sleeping animals.

"Texas country is at its best during the night. It's not at all like New Orleans," she commented unexpectedly. "That city comes alive at night; this land sleeps and rejuvenates itself for the next day. It offers rest for those who battle the elements. New Orleans is like going without sleep for long periods of time."

"Tell me about your aunt Lucille."

Sally smiled while her mind whisked her back to simpler times. "My aunt was the gentlest person I knew in New Orleans. She basked in every moment of life and found joy in everyone surrounding her. She never allowed me to get discouraged and quietly reminded me of the good in everyone. We had a very special bond." Sally turned toward Adam, the man who—after all—helped her learn to ride as a child, coached her with 4-H, and drove all her junior high friends to any place in the county they wanted to go. She loved Adam for making her life bearable and she loved Aunt Lucille for making her life meaningful.

Adam's eyes empathetically stared into Sally's as he interpreted her thoughts. He slowly veered from the road and stopped the truck, yanking on the emergency break. He wrapped his large arm around her burdened shoulders. Perhaps it was the feeling of completeness, or the contentment and peace, or maybe it was all of the welcome feelings wrapped up together that Sally and Adam took from each other—what was needed to satisfy them individually at that moment. When peace and acceptance are so readily available, no one should pass up the opportunity to take advantage.

"What I'm going to tell you requires a bit of understanding on your part, Sally," Adam finally broke the silence.

"Just be straight with me. That's all I've ever asked."

"Okay. That's fair. This all begins with the fact that the Straight S Ranch is corporate owned."

"I know that. Most all large ranches need the capital from large corporations these days to survive the hard times—except yours, I suppose—I remember when Dad reminisced about the Straight S being signed over from the original owner. My dad seemed very sad about a generation lost, but without that corporate capital, especially during the recent drought, the ranch would not have had the cash to sustain itself. He told me the Straight S was the very first ranch in Texas to legally be owned in this manner. I believe the action set a precedent," Sally said flippantly.

Adam sighed. "If you will let me finish... About five years ago some old deeds were discovered which questioned ownership of the Straight S." Adam chose his words carefully. "Certain arrangements were essential if the Straight S were to be preserved, so to speak. Legally, these arrangements satisfied the letter of the law, but moral ramifications to certain actions have a way of resurfacing at inopportune times. The deeds themselves were questionable. It was a situation where hundreds of people would lose out on something they'd invested their lives in. Success for many people in this world is a contentment to be a part of something they don't actually own and contribute to its growth and success."

"But you and I aren't two of those people, are we?"

"Sorry. I didn't mean to imply that your ambitions were any less than mine. Anyway, your father approached me one day and told me all about this plan he had to preserve the Straight S..."

"Who found these documents?" Sally interrupted.

"James Wright."

"The Mr. Wright that died several years ago?"

"Five."

"Mrs. Wright's Mr. Wright?" she asked, astonished. " No wonder you were upset when I was asking her questions about your land in the real estate office! But what does your ranch have to do with all of this, and what was my father's plan?"

"Before I continue with my explanation, I'm going to tell you right now that this has absolutely nothing to do with my ranch. Hamilton Ranch is mine, free and clear."

"Don't be defensive. I wasn't implying anything. So what about my father's plan to preserve the Straight S? It obviously worked."

"The plan was necessary because we both know that government subsidies are essential to the farmer's and rancher's survival, corporate capital or not. Five years ago, the government disallowed the planting of maize, among other crops, which are the lifeline of the ranch. Millions of acres were to lie dormant. You know the drill. The government pays to not plant and the ranch survives, the price of grain stays on an even keel, and whenever the government deems it necessary we get to again plant maize and other crops. But, because of the questionable ownership of the land, the paperwork your dad sent to the government for the subsidies came hurling back to him like a Texas tornado. Because he would not be reimbursed by the government meant the loss of capital needed to survive. Your dad felt that if he could temporarily sell the titles of several parcels of land to people who worked on the ranch and then buy them back when things were cleared up, the government would be satisfied."

"The Straight S cheated the government? Are you talking fraud?"

"No. Stop assuming the worst. Listen to the whole story."

"The more you explain the more confused I seem to get."

"Then just listen. You'll understand when I'm finished. Now, to emphasize my earlier point—at no time whatsoever did the Straight S cheat the government. What your dad did was to deed parcels of land to many of the ranch hands who had spent their lives on the Straight S—about twenty thousand acres apiece. He applied for subsidies under these people's names and received his money, but he would have received that same money from the government even if the land had continued to be corporate owned. It was a big gamble, but he won. Ownership was not questioned."

"The corporation agreed to this?"

"What choice did they have? It would have meant the loss of millions of dollars. Corporations have capital but not enough to sustain the largest ranch in Texas raking in only half of its possible income. And who knows how many years the government would not have allowed these certain crops to be planted?"

"I think I understand now why you entered politics. These are issues no one would understand unless they had a stake in them. Well, who was the shady owner who couldn't receive the government subsidies?"

"It was your dad."

"What?" Sally was astonished.

"Your father said he did it as a favor for someone many years ago and he never thought it would be questioned, but ranching has changed, with government intervention, rules, and regulations. All taxes and moneys were received through the corporation, but when the government saw that there might possibly be double-registered ownership—the corporation and your father—fraud was the first thing the government considered. They felt as though your dad might try to receive a double subsidy."

"So my dad's name was on the deed to the Straight S. My father knows why he did someone a favor."

"I'm sure, but I never asked him. I figured it was his business, and I respected his privacy. I still do."

"What does Bill Tans have to do with this?"

"He received money for using his name. Everyone did. The deeds were in the process of being transferred back when you arrived home. I suppose that could have been the air of secrecy you felt."

"Five years—you're right. The ranch would not have survived."

"But what does Bill want now?"

"Something for nothing, like so many people these days. He seems to feel he put his name on the line for a large corporation and that he deserves more than what he originally received. Actually, he's trying to blackmail your father."

"Blackmail? That's pretty harsh."

"He said that if your dad didn't give him more money, he would tell the government about the deeds, and, even if he didn't have a leg to stand on, the Straight S holdings and assets would be held up in court for years. Business could be nonexistent for a period of time the ranch may not be able to withstand. What would you call it?"

"Okay. But I'm still confused. What I don't understand is how Mr. Wright found out about the deeds."

"Land titles are a matter of public record. Perhaps Mr. Wright was looking for land to buy, stumbled across the names, and mentioned it to the wrong people. I don't know."

"I wonder why my father's name was on those deeds."

"Your father asked me to trust him. I told you. I didn't ask him questions."

"And you were satisfied with that?"

"Yes. And I still am."

"Well, I'm not. There's more to this than meets the eye. You're telling me my father's name was on the deed to the Straight S, along with a corporation that owns it. Why? It doesn't make any sense. And what about my mother's letters and my aunt telling me to ask my father why he sent me away for five years, which he blatantly denies now?"

"Five years ago all this mess started about the deeds. Perhaps he didn't want you in the middle of it all."

"I hardly think so."

"Think what you might. I thought you would be satisfied to hear the truth."

"Perhaps if it was the whole truth."

"Why don't you just trust your father?"

"It's not a matter of trust. And, honestly, I can't understand why you would be satisfied either, unless you know more than what you're telling me."

"There isn't any more to explain now. The simple fact of the matter is that the government saw a corporate name and your father's name on the deed to the ranch and questioned the fact that your father might try to receive a double payment from the government to abstain from growing certain crops. He changed names on some deeds. That's the end of the story. Come on. You need your sleep."

"I can't let this go. I can't. I plan to make this town my home, and I'm not going to build a future here on lies." Sally shifted uneasily. "I have an appointment with Mrs. Wright tomorrow, and I'm going to ask her a lot of questions. I'm also going to the county seat in Addison and look up some old records."

"Sally, trust me. You always have in the past. Don't go to Addison. It has nothing to do with you."

"I'm going to find out why you met me in town to reminisce."

"You're talking crazy again."

"Yeah, right. I don't think that word should be said lightly."

Adam started up the engine. As they drove up to the house, John walked out and met them at the truck window. "Ya'll doing okay?" He glanced at Adam and then at Sally.

"Everything's fine, John. Give us a minute, will you?"

Adam turned toward Sally. "Give it a rest tonight. We're all tired, and everything will seem different in the morning. Don't waste your time in Addison."

"The only thing that will seem different in the morning is the sky and its reflection on those windmills sleeping on the horizon." Sally pushed open the door and slammed it shut.

Sally's gaze followed Adam's vehicle down the drive until the red lights disappeared. "So, Adam, if everything is so simple, why did you hire Tans away from the Straight S?" she asked to the dusty trail.

Sally's father was in the kitchen pouring himself a cup of coffee. "You wanna join me?" he asked without turning around.

"I want to talk, Dad."

"I presume Adam told you about the deeds. Well, don't hold it against me. We all do what we think is right at the time. We would have gotten the money anyway, Sally. I didn't cheat the government. Believe me, my interests weren't my first priority. There were a lot of people's lives at stake. But this will work out. I'm sure Tans won't bother you again. He didn't hurt you, did he?"

"He scared me, Dad. Isn't that enough to tell me everything that is going on?"

"Ain't nothing more to say. He's a drunk and an old fool."

"So why is he Adam's assistant foreman?"

John gulped the last of his coffee and rinsed his cup in the sink. "I don't know. I suppose Tans is good at what he does. I'm going to bed. I feel awfully tired tonight."

"Dad, you've been tired an awful lot lately. Are you sick?"

"Naw." John shuffled to his room.

Sally continued to sit in the kitchen alone, thinking about her father and the distance they'd always had. She couldn't recall a time when any conversation between them was longer than ten minutes, but she knew her father loved her. It was just his way.

The 2:00 a.m. feeding of the calf passed without incident, as did the 6:00 a.m. and 10:00 a.m. Al was flourishing, and many a rancher for miles around visited that morning to view the new breed of cow which would double their profits in the future and weather the most violent conditions Texas had to offer. Sally beamed with pride at every visit but lacked energy to show her enthusiasm. She could not manipulate any more information from her father. Around ten thirty she headed for the real estate office to see Mrs. Wright. The vet was scheduled to check the calf after she returned from Addison. Her own hectic schedule was causing her to feel a bit edgy all the time. She snapped at people more often than not, and she was sick of apologizing for it.

Mrs. Wright's conversation about Sally's mother was in no way revealing except for the fact that her moodiness was apparent to all who lived in the town, especially toward the end. When she asked Mrs. Wright about Adam and her husband, she was cut off abruptly. Sally felt an uneasiness about the woman and wondered why she had suddenly changed her attitude. Then, to top it off, Mrs. Wright's prospects of land parcels dwindled down to only one bit of property. She told Sally the prospective sellers would not consider owner financing after all, despite the information on the computer printout. Times were hard, and they needed the cash. Sally also discovered that she'd lost the letters from her mother and her own computer printout the morning she walked out to the corral to retrieve her purse, which she had carelessly flung on the fence post the night before. She figured they were lost to the Texas wind and regretted sticking the computer printout and the letters in the side pocket of her purse.

Mrs. Wright explained that the land was a fifty-acre parcel located next to the Straight S, and Sally wondered why the corporation had not already purchased it. It even had an old house sitting on it in deplorable condition and fixing it up, she thought, would be a future commitment. Sally planned to secure the fences first so she could bring her two horses out to graze. The barn was an old cow barn, but with a little bit of ingenuity she could manipulate some temporary horse stalls. All in all, she considered herself extremely lucky for there was a low down payment, owner financing, and the papers could be drawn up within days making her, at last, a landowner. She was even allowed to begin fixing up the property right away and was elated when she returned to the Straight S. Her fatigue miraculously dissipated and she immediately attended her duties making the rounds on the ranch. It was still a solid two hours before she would have to feed Al again; maybe she could even catch an hour of sleep. She was also excited about going to Addison that afternoon, but that would be a close one. It was a forty-minute drive to the county seat alone. If she had been shirking her duties that day her father had not mentioned it. In fact, he seemed to be avoiding her somewhat, electing to eat out on the range instead of coming home at noon, many times missing the evening meal as well.

On the trip to Addison Sally enjoyed the unreliable air conditioning system in an early model car. She usually drove the truck, but its use was essential on the ranch that day so she reluctantly drove one of the older vehicles. The coolness inside the old station wagon blew against her wet face, and she removed her hat, allowing the refrigerated air to do its job thoroughly. Her jeans were dusty and her long-sleeved cotton shirt showed signs of a full day's work on the ranch already. Sally removed the clip from her hair, and her long waves slowly made their way down her back. *I am a landowner,* she thought contentedly and felt an obligation to write Aunt Lucille and thank her for making her save the money from her part-time job in New Orleans. Because Aunt Lucille hadn't written or called lately, Sally decided to make it a point to contact her that evening and engage in one of their hour-long chats.

The air conditioning had sufficiently refreshed Sally's body and soul as she stepped into the nineteenth-century brick courthouse. A young girl behind a desk directed her to the cases that housed the cumbersome books of hand-recorded deeds. Deeds were a matter of public record so they were available to anyone who wished to review the over-bound documents. She wondered how her father had legally been able to be on record synonymously with a corporation as owner-ship of the ranch. After an hour of searching to no avail, Sally's frustration led her to the desk for help. The perky girl quickly informed her they were not allowed to assist but that one of the higher clerks in the next office might have the information she needed.

A knock on the door and a brief apology of disturbance earned Sally a seat in front of an efficient-looking bookkeeper. He was an awkward little man working feverishly on his computer.

"May I help you?" he asked, without looking up.

"Yes, I've been searching through the deed books in the outer office, and there seems to be some information missing. The deeds to the Straight S Ranch dating about twenty-two to twenty-five years ago are not there."

The clerk grew a patronizing grin. "I assure you, they are there. Perhaps you have the location confused—for example, the farm road number. Road names and numbers change, especially if the county comes in and, well, takes them over, you see."

"I'm sure the roads were not changed. I've lived here all my life, and no numbers on the signs—"

"Excuse me for interrupting"—the man smiled—"but sometimes it takes a while for the maintenance to catch up to the paperwork. For example, what we in the office refer to as 'segment 1604' may be the 'Williamson survey of 1929' to everyone else. The county sent in a number of clerks and private lawyers about five years ago to sup-posedly reconstruct the system to make it easier to locate—"

"Can't you just find it for me?" Sally interrupted.

"I am a bit busy at the moment, but if you'll come back this after-noon...just leave me the information and I'll look for it."

"I cannot come back this afternoon."

"All right. Let me see what I can do."

Sally nervously scanned the clock on the wall as the man meticu-lously searched book after book. She felt the urgency of returning home before the vet would arrive to check out Al.

"I don't understand it. There does seem to be some missing doc-uments." He flipped through some pages. "Sections are definitely gone. I have told these people over and over again that parts cannot be removed; whole books have to be checked out and are never to leave this building. What if they are lost?" He stared at Sally.

"I don't know." She wondered if he really expected an answer.

The man rushed to his desk. "And according to the list, only the Frasier Book is checked out to Office #3. This is all very confusing."

Sally could no longer wait. "I really do have to go. I appreciate your time and effort. I'll just have to come back another day." As Sally pushed open the door to the hallway, the young office girl cautiously approached her. She steered Sally to the side and spoke in a low voice.

"I couldn't help but overhear your conversation. I don't know what it is you're looking for, but my boss did get a call from Representative Hamilton this morning—you know, our new 23rd

District Representative. He was asking the same questions you were just now. I know because my boss records his phone calls and I type them up for his records. You seem so desperate. I believe the records were pulled and sent to his office as a… well, you know, a personal favor. Perhaps Representative Hamilton has the answers you need. You can reach him through the state capitol, or his local office is located in Benning."

"Thank you."

The girl smiled and returned to her desk.

"What kind of power does a district representative have to pull county records at request over the telephone?" Sally murmured. Well, obviously, it was the kind of power she lacked.

Of course, Sally blamed the decadent use of the air conditioning to explain the breakdown of the old car. It was her indulgence in luxuries. She silently recriminated herself for thinking so Victorian, but Al needed to be fed in just an hour and she was drowning in guilt. Sally was forced to telephone her father to explain why she wouldn't be available for the vet and then asked him to make arrangements with Karen to feed the little calf with the vet tech present. He said he guessed he would also handle the car situation.

An hour later, Adam pulled up to the curb in front of the courthouse. Being double-parked, he couldn't leave the vehicle. Sally hesitantly walked to the truck and got in. "Did you lock the car?" Adam asked without looking at her.

"The car is locked."

"A few of the boys are coming up after work to get it running and bring it home. Give me the keys."

"Are they Hamilton or Straight—"

"Does it make a bit of difference?"

"This is Straight S business."

"It's everybody's business when things are neglected. The boys can fix the car."

"The way you fixed it in the county clerk's office so I couldn't find any old deeds? Just what kind of power do you have that you can pull strings in the county courthouse?"

"All district representatives have clout. It's part of the package."

"Whose side are you on, anyway?"

"There are no sides. What exactly were you expecting to find?"

"Answers. I'm looking for straight answers." Sally's lack of accomplishment at the County Seat, the breaking down of the car, the lack of sleep, the frustration of her dependence upon others all pressed upon her as she sat in the front of the truck, no escape possible. Her eyes burned as tears began to form and spill down her cheeks. Her tired body began to shake as her hands covered the face of a woman too tired to fight. Adam sighed, leaned back in his seat, and pulled Sally toward him.

"You're not so tough, you know."

"Obviously you're not either."

Adam laughed. "Touché. There's a pizza place down the road with a buffet. Let's stop and eat. It's too late for you to feed Al anyway, and the vet has already come and gone."

Sally groaned. She'd let herself down today as well as everyone around her. She sat pensively while Adam drove.

As Adam paid for the pizza, Sally freshened up in the bathroom. She stared at herself in the mirror and sighed.

They both waited in a short line and loaded up with various kinds of pizza and salad. After an agonizing stint of silence, Sally finally spoke.

"I want to apologize for crying earlier."

"Why? You don't have to apologize for honest emotions. Hell, I don't apologize for anything, almost."

"I'm just tired and frustrated."

"Why don't you just concentrate on Al for a while?"

"And forget my wild goose chases? I would probably be satisfied right now if it weren't for you."

"I doubt it."

"Lord! You see how you talk to me? In stupid riddles…"

"I admit I asked for the records. They are being sent to my office. I don't know what's in those records either. They may affect me too, Sally. I don't want to lose what I have built in my lifetime. I think you can imagine what my ranch means to me. You may be hurting a lot of people. I need to look at the records first."

"You don't trust me?"

"Look who's talking."

"Can't we look at them together?"

"No."

"Adam, just how powerful is a district representative from Texas? Or is it just because your name is Adam Hamilton?"

"I hope you don't find out the hard way."

"Is that a threat?"

"Can you honestly tell me you can't sense how I feel about you by what I am willing to do for you? I could never threaten you. I could threaten those around you to make you have a better world, or I could threaten Bobby March when he said he was going to beat you up when you received that first place ribbon in that barrel racing competition."

Sally sat up straight. "Is that why twelve-year-old icky freckled-face Bobby March apologized to me on his knees?" Sally reminisced. "You made him get on his knees and tell me he was sorry? God, Adam, did you make him send me those flowers every day for two weeks in a row?" Sally laughed in disbelief.

"I had to protect my up-and-coming seventh grader." Adam sighed. "Well, tell me he didn't deserve it."

"He deserved it." Sally felt overwhelmed with emotion. "He deserved it. He was the biggest rat in school."

"Then case closed."

"How many others?"

Adam jumped up from the table and headed for the door. He turned back to Sally. "I wouldn't touch that question with a ten-foot pole."

That evening Sally, in-between feedings, decided to make good on her promise to call Aunt Lucille in New Orleans. Perhaps her aunt could shed a little welcome light on the mysteries in her life. John slammed the screen door as he ceremoniously walked in the house. Having not seen him all day, Sally desperately wanted to hear about the vet's visit. She placed the receiver back on the phone after letting it ring only a few times.

John passed her and headed straight into the kitchen to get a pitcher of water out of the refrigerator and a glass from the cupboard.

Sitting wearily at the chair he poured himself a drink. He looked up as Sally walked in. "I thought you were on the phone. I didn't want to disturb you."

"I was calling Aunt Lucille. It can wait."

"Your aunt?"

"Yeah. You hungry, Dad?"

"Yes, as a matter of fact, I am. How about heating up some of that roast and potatoes?"

"Sure. It will give us a chance to talk."

"Sally…"

"I just want to know what the vet said about Al. I'm sorry I wasn't here. Dad, I want you to know I feel really badly about Al. I know how important he is. I won't miss another feeding or visit from the vet again. I promise. I'll never let you down again. Please, what did he have to say?"

"Said everything was fine. He said you were a good mother. Said you would make a fine heifer." He grinned uncharacteristically.

"Thank God!" Sally hadn't seen him smile in a long time. "I bought some land adjacent to the Straight S." Sally heated up the food. "It's fifty acres of good pasture. Thought I'd check the fences out this weekend, maybe put Lady Grace and Lord Johnson out to graze. Thought I could practice my barrel racing out there. It has a cow barn. I can convert it into a horse…"

Sally's dad was not listening to her anymore. The faraway gaze lit up his eyes as he peered out of the kitchen window, the windmills resting from the heated day. A tear slowly rolled down Sally's cheek as she watched him sitting so still in the chair. Her father appeared so tired these days. But he was tough, and whatever it was that was bothering him, he would survive. She was sure of that.

CHAPTER FOUR

Windmills lay among the grass.
Tornadoes spread a path.
The sky's been bare for many days
While farmers fix God's wrath.

Metal cuts beneath the soil
As each drops to the ground.
Noises echo through the hills,
A shrilling, crashing sound.

The next morning hailed warmth and serenity. The temperature was
not yet battling the air so the windmills and trees sat dormant, anticipating the morning's first movement. Al was faring well and everyone decided that Sally did indeed know what she was doing, despite
the acquisition of fifty acres. When she finished her duties on the
Straight S, she proceeded to her future home and began mending
fences. It was a slow, painful process as she resisted offerings from
Adam and the hands. It might have been pride, but Sally's goals she
had set when she stepped on Texas soil were clear—she could manage her life alone. She was eager to set her two horses loose on her
land as soon as possible as she desperately needed to acquire a sense
of belonging and ownership accomplished that goal.

While Sally stretched barbed wire near her cow barn, Adam drove up in his truck. She was sweaty yet invigorated, feeling her newly acquired chore was labor for her own land and not someone else's. She smiled at his presence, temporarily forgetting about the deeds and the mystery surrounding the Straight S. Sally's sense of contentment ruled her thoughts and she removed the heavy gloves to retrieve some liquid from the water cooler perched on the tailgate of the truck.

"Have some water? Tastes great on a day like this." Sally filled her cup and drank greedily, spilling some down her chin. She smiled and wiped the water from her face, smudging the country dirt across her cheek.

"Why don't you also get a full-time job in town to fill up your spare time at night?" Adam studied his surroundings.

Sally sighed and filled her cup once again. "I told you I was going to do this. I'm not in seventh grade anymore. I know my limits, but, more importantly, I know what is best for me. I want to put my horses out to pasture here as soon as possible. Look at these great grasses!" Sally gazed upon her land much like her father did every morning of his life. "It'll all burn up in a month or so, you know. I want Lady Grace and Lord Johnson to be able to graze as long as possible. This coastal looks as though it was seeded this past winter, and there are so few weeds that the brush hasn't even had a chance to come out yet. You can tell it's been mowed quite often. I was pretty lucky to get this land at a decent price."

"It's only fifty acres—hardly enough to look at with pride."

"Well, it's my fifty acres, isn't it? And you can't tell me you didn't feel the exact same way I do now every time you acquired every bit of acreage for your ranch." Sally yanked her heavy gloves into place. "I've got work to do."

"It'll get dark really fast now that the sun has set behind the hills."

"Don't worry. I'll feed Al on time."

"I'm thinking it's not safe here after dark."

"Why not? Are the snakes packing guns these days?"

Adam was suddenly too serious. "This isn't a joke. Sit for a minute. I need to talk to you."

"Okay. Shoot." Sally and Adam perched beneath the shade of an old, gnarly mesquite tree, Sally resting her aching back against the rough trunk. She removed her gloves once again and slapped them against her boot.

"I think you should have a hand out here if you're going to be working after dark, and I'd like to help you with the fencing and such."

"Why? Sounds like you hate what I'm doing. I really can't understand why you would offer to help fix up my 'prideless' land."

"I'm offering you help as one neighbor to another—you know, me being a familiar neighbor…"

"So you remember trivial conversations that happened a long time ago in a small field in Benning, Texas. But the real question here is do you know how to properly mend the typical Texas barbed wire fence with its mesquite posts and hot wires challenging the most capable men… and women of course?"

"Ownership does make you happy… and forgiving."

"Adam, don't you see? I'm making my dreams come true. It's such an awesome feeling. You had to have felt like this so many times…"

"Well, can you use help?"

"I really wanted to do it myself—you know the feeling of pride… but if you're going to help for the right reasons… Although it is peaceful out here doing things my way…"

Sally didn't have a chance to complete her thoughts. Adam grabbed her gloves and tossed her his truck keys. "Here, take these and back up my truck as close to that post as possible. We'll finish stretching this wire tonight." Sally didn't hesitate. She jumped into the truck and backed it up close to Adam. He secured the wires to the vehicle with a "come-a-long," and Sally carefully pressed the gas pedal, allowing the truck to slowly pull and stretch while Adam hammered the staples into the posts to secure the barbed metal. They repeated the routine over and over until the stretch of fence line was secure.

"All right!" Adam yelled. "That's enough. You can cut me some slack now. This last bit ought to hold."

"That was fast. I suppose there is something to be said for brawn. Too bad this isn't the only spot that needs fixing. But that will have to wait until tomorrow. I've got to get back to the ranch and feed Al."

Sally loaded all of her supplies in the back of the truck with Adam's help and asked him over for supper. She was bursting with contentment.

The aroma of pork chops filled the house as Sally cooked while Adam sat on a stool in the kitchen taking turns watching her and flipping through the *Texas Stockman*.

"Al was easy to feed tonight, wasn't he? But I know he's not out of danger, even now. I gave him another injection last night as he seemed to sleep longer than usual, but he's trying out those new legs and all..."

"I looked over those deeds today."

Sally didn't respond or turn to meet Adam's gaze. She plopped the cut potatoes into the boiling water on the stove.

"There was nothing unusual about the recordings. Your father's name was on them, and that's all."

"But before my father's and the corporation, whose name was on the deeds?"

"Captain King, of course. He owned the land before the corporation bought it. You know he was the original owner of the ranch."

"Of, course. That's Texas History 101. I thought maybe there was someone else, you know, in between."

"Nope."

"Ahh, the famous Captain King. I haven't thought about him in a long time. There wouldn't be any town around here if it wasn't for him or any productive ranches. If I remember correctly, he originally bought all of these thousands of acres and began the Straight S even before the railroads were built. What a gamble! But who asked my father to put his name on those deeds? What is the actual recorded name of the corporation on the deeds?" The cracking and popping of the grease became louder.

"Your father's name was always there in conjunction with a holding company. There was only a number listed each time beside his name. That is all that's required, you know. I checked the legal ramifications."

"Then I'll just have to ask my dad."

"I don't know if that's a good idea."

"Why not?"

"Don't you think he would have told you if he wanted you to know? Maybe you should just trust him and his decisions."

Sally flipped the chops and turned down the boiling potatoes. "You know something, don't you? You gave me your word that you would help me."

"I'm not going against my word. All the recorded books had to offer was what I told you."

"Then you know something that you didn't get from those books."

"I told you what you wanted to know. Whatever knowledge you think I have other than the information I got from those books is my own business."

Sally stood silent until the dinner finished cooking. She couldn't even look at Adam without feeling angry and helpless. Finally, she couldn't help herself. "Well, thank you for your help. It will be the last time I ask."

Sally's father stepped into the kitchen. "What's going on?" He shuffled over to the refrigerator and grasped a cold drink. "You two mad at each other?"

"So you find our situation amusing? You two think you have all the answers don't you? Fine. Why don't ya'll both sit and eat together and talk about all the little secrets you share between the two of you." Sally threw the chops and potatoes into the bowls and slammed the dishes on the table. "I'm not hungry. But by all means, ya'll help yourselves."

Sally sulked in her room, feeling as though she had no dignity at all. One minute Adam helped her mend fences, building her pride in the land she'd bought, and the next minute he stripped her of that pride, making her feel insignificant and inconsequential. How cruel fate was sometimes. As it gives, it also takes away. Sally watched the trail of dust from her bedroom window as Adam drove away.

She heard no more until her alarm went off at 10:00 p.m. for Al's feeding. Groaning, Sally halfheartedly lifted herself out of bed. It was a good thing she always preset her clock for the next feeding. She did so again, automatically setting it for 2:00 a.m. Even though Sally had been on this feeding schedule before, she never felt the pressure she did with Al. Allowing a hand to take over some of the feedings at night was routine with a regular calf, but Al was special and Sally wanted to be sure he thrived under her care. Perhaps she felt she had something to prove, but mostly she loved the little fellow so much that the thought of losing him was unbearable at this point.

The kitchen presented itself as though it was dinner time, except the chops and potatoes were put away. Sally knew Adam hadn't eaten, but only a closer inspection of the food would tell her whether her father did. She was too exhausted to care at the moment. But, always planning ahead, she smiled to herself, thinking she wouldn't have to cook much of a breakfast in the morning, just scramble a few eggs to go along with the chops. Sally also made the coffee and set the timer to be ready at 5:00 a.m. She moaned to herself at the thought of getting up again in just a few hours.

Sally stumbled into Al's pen and roused him with the noise of the buckets and bottles. He scrambled up on all fours, bawling and licking her face as she nuzzled up to his nose. He instantly sucked from the bottle as Sally stroked his smooth brown-and-white hide, sleek in the moonlight. She routinely listened to his lungs and again gave him his regular injection of antibiotics—a constant battle to keep pneumonia from setting in. The little calf had just been given another injection from the vet tech but didn't seem to mind the shots. Sally decided that Al was finally ready for an outing and soon she would collar and leash him for a walk in the grasses. She sighed at the thought. She actually wished she could be content to stay on the Straight S, but a feeling deep inside would not allow her the luxury. She leaned on the cedar posts of the gate as she carried the buckets and bottles out of the pen. The moon was full, illuminating Adam's house, tiny specks of steady brightness below the hills. She wondered what his role was to be in her future. Between Al, the ranch, and her new place time had become her enemy.

Breakfast was uneventful; her father asked about Al, and then told her to get more rest during the day. He announced the vet would be out at 10:00 a.m. Sally was more than a little anxious to hear what the doctor was going to tell her as she remembered with regret how she had missed his last visit when the car broke down in Addison.

Dr. Lopez worked slowly and meticulously as he checked out the young calf's heart, ears, and other vital parts. He laughed as Al curled up in Sally's lap during the examination. Whenever Dr.

Lopez needed him to walk, Sally led him around the pen, the young calf keenly aware of her every move.

"Do you have time for some coffee or tea while you're here?" Sally asked as they left the corral. The doctor was a young man and, according to her dad, had returned to the area immediately after graduating from vet school two years before. John liked him because he'd grown up on a ranch close to Benning and said he had "common sense" doctoring as well as the knowledge of an educated man. He was the only vet her dad called anymore "from the outside," knowing his mobile unit was well-equipped. The Straight S had its own full-time vet on staff, but his specialty was horses and Dr. Lopez worked wonders with cattle.

"I guess I'll take a cool glass of anything you have," he said, smiling. "Already it must be 85 degrees." He spoke with an accent and sometimes Sally found it hard to understand his English. It seemed today as though he was taking an inordinate amount of time before revealing the results of his examination. "He's doing okay."

"Just okay? What does that mean?"

"Okay is good," he reassured her. "Keep doing the same as what you are doing now."

"Do you think he'll develop into a normal, fully grown, functional bull?"

"Ask me again in about twelve months."

"But he's doing well?"

"We can give injections and feed him, but if he wasn't ready to be here…"

"But he's walking…"

"Instinct."

"You're not going to tell me anything encouraging?"

"It is like the first time I was here. He's doing okay."

Adam drove up as the vet was descending the porch stairs, not even acknowledging Sally before he and the doctor began discussing the calf's progress. She grew tired of watching them and left for the kitchen to stir up some lunch. She needed the confirmation that she had done a wonderful job so far and no one could have done what she had accomplished.

Adam walked in as she sat down at the table setting a plate and drink before her.

"Your father said to tell you he wasn't coming home for lunch."

"I didn't fix him anything," she snapped. "That's his usual routine these days."

"Don't kill the messenger."

"You want a sandwich?" When she started to get up Adam placed a hand on her shoulder.

"I'll get it." He stared at Sally while fixing his meal. "Did Al have a bad night? You look tired."

"No, he didn't have a bad night. Actually he was in a playful mood, so we stayed up talking, the two of us, about life and its spikes and pitfalls. We talked about honesty and trust."

"That must have been a one-way conversation." Adam sat down. "The vet said—"

"Nothing."

"He said Al was doing fine."

"Yeah, I suppose." Sally and Adam ate their sandwiches in silence. "I'm going to lie down for a while. I've got a few deliveries and pay-roll, but I don't think I can keep my eyes open another second."

Adam accompanied Sally into the bedroom and sat on the side of the bed. "I could use some rest myself, you know."

"Are you suggesting—"

"Sleep."

"Yeah, right. I just need to rest for a little while. I'm too tired to harbor evil thoughts," Sally whispered as she closed her eyes.

"I'll take Al's next feeding." Sally didn't hear Adam, as she had already fallen asleep. Adam reached over to the faded alarm clock and pressed the button. He opened the squeaky window, and the afternoon breeze gently pushed itself into the room, summer noises mingled with the odor of the fields. The creaking metal of the wind-mills filled the room, but did not disturb Sally's slumber.

The five o'clock dinner bell for the temporary summer ranch hands rang obtrusively, jarring Sally from her sleep. She read Adam's note about feeding Al at 2:00. Feeling drugged, Sally stumbled out of bed and headed toward the holding pen. Al was walking around the tiny corral, inspecting the hanging wooden pails with his large, black nose. She wondered how Adam had done with the feeding and turned to go in the house to prepare the calf's food. Since sleeping most of the day, Sally decided to feed Al and then take him for a walk in the fields beyond the pastures where no other cows grazed. She remembered Adam told her the ranch hands always practiced for the rodeo on the eastern section of his ranch. She would drive Al out there in the truck and then walk him below the hills. She lamented her absent time needed to practice for the barrel racing event and this way she could observe the cowboys, take Al where she was sure no other cattle were grazing and get out in the open for a while. She basked in the spring and summer months and the fact that it didn't get dark until 9:00 p.m. Payroll could wait until tomorrow, and she presumed her dad's foreman took care of the deliveries. Life went on.

Al took a halter fairly well as he trusted Sally, but she also hooked him up while he was eating which aided his accommodating attitude immensely. She packed the cell phone in addition to the car phone in case she needed help when she walked Al away from the truck. Sally wasn't going to take any chances with history in the making. One of the hands along with the vet tech hoisted Al in the truck and secured him firmly with the lead rope. Sally drove cautiously down the dirt road of the ranch, absorbing its serene atmosphere and enjoying every precious second the Texas summer had to offer. She casually waved to some of the workers who were mending fences and others who were checking out some cattle. The Straight S was a world all its own and functioned with the aid of hundreds of different people, including her. She realized she had already received assistance with her measly fifty acres and temporarily admitted that no one can do it all alone.

Sally eased the brakes of the truck at the bottom of the hills where Adam had mentioned earlier their two ranches adjoined. Hollering and yelling echoed through the valley between the hills. She smiled, spotting the men practicing their bull riding. She unloaded the calf and, to Sally's delight, Al began a bit of grazing as he wobbled through unfamiliar territory. Sally's delight extended while watching the cowboys jeering and laughing, especially when one of them narrowly escaped the wrath of a bull. She desperately needed to practice for that barrel racing competition that was coming up soon. Sally leaned up against the barbed barrier between the ranches until Al became restless and began backing up, tugging on his lead rope. Sally led him to greener pastures. They explored farther than she thought Al capable, and, as Sally perched on a rock to rest, a truck unexpectedly jerked to a halt beside her.

A sudden fear engulfed her as Bill Tans narrowly missed both of them. The small calf's eyes widened in fear, and he bucked at the nearness of the truck. "Are you crazy?" Sally screamed. "You could have killed us!"

Tans slowly opened the creaky truck door, his smile widening as he slid out. "Well, I suppose I just stumbled onto a gold mine. I reckoned that truck back yonder looked familiar as I passed by. I guess I was right on target in putting it out of commission for a while. Seems you've wandered far off the trail, and there's no one out here except me and you. I also took care of this phone here so that we won't be disturbed." He held up the smashed car phone and let it drop to the ground. He slithered uncomfortably close to Sally, and she stumbled back toward the trunk of a large tree, her grip tightening on Al's leash.

"There are some hands just past the fence practicing for the rodeo!" Sally screamed nervously.

"Seems like you better look again, girlie. I believe you wandered away from them a long time ago. They couldn't hear you now if you shouted at the top of those pretty little lungs of yours, and even if they did the echo in these hills would throw them off the track. They'd be looking for hours." Tans laughed, exposing tobacco-stained teeth as he spit on the ground.

"What do you want?" Sally demanded.

"What do you want? What do you want?" Bill mockingly repeated Sally's words. "I want what's mine!" he yelled to the hills, proving to Sally that no one could hear them and that he didn't care. "I've kept silent for a long time now and I think my information is worth more than what I got for it."

"A lot of people were involved with changing their names on those deeds so the Straight S could start operating. They don't want more money. What makes you so special?"

Tans roared with laughter and staggered back from Sally, relieving the tension a bit. "Is that what your daddy told you?" He glared at her. "That's really rich. Now all that ain't quite true and there's an even better part to tell."

"What do you mean?"

"Well, now, I don't think it would hurt anything if I said it out loud. It won't change the fact that your papa is a murderer. Who do you think done in poor 'ol Mr. Wright?"

Sally's heartbeat quickened but she was stunned silent for just seconds before her verbal retaliation. "You're a liar and a drunken, stinkin' old fool!"

Al began bawling, Sally having jerked on his leash as she lashed out at Bill. Tans only laughed and wiped his grungy mouth.

Sally quickly gathered her thoughts. "Mr. Wright died of a heart attack five years ago. Everyone knows that."

"A heart attack, huh? Pretty convenient, don't you think? He finds out about those deeds, and not more than a week later he's dead. I don't know what that spells in your book, but in mine, it's murder."

"It's a coincidence, that's all."

"Then why did your dad give me more money than the rest when I mentioned my 'coincidence' to him?" Tans laughed, wheezing and coughing at the same time, sounding more and more sinister as his story progressed.

"I don't know and I don't care. You're nothing but a liar and a drunk, and I need to get back home." Sally tried to sound calm. Her thoughts raced to the cell phone she had retrieved from her backpack when Tans's eyes were averted by Al's erratic behavior. She quickly pressed the speed dial to the ranch. Before Tans knew what she was doing, Adam's voice echoed from the fragile lifeline. Both glared at it simultaneously and, before Sally could speak, he stole it from her and smashed it onto the rocks, splitting the electronic device open and rendering it useless. The sound echoed ominously in the hills harmonizing with the windmills' retaliation to the Texas heat. Sally tried to push her way past him, but Tans snatched her arm and yanked her right up to his sweaty, filthy clothes. Instinctively, she kept a tight hold on Al, the leash scraping her hands raw as the horrified calf kept backing away from the two of them struggling, his brown eyes still wide from terror.

"Let me go!" Sally screamed and kicked Tans in the leg, desperately trying to escape. His grip loosened as she yanked free, allowing her to temporarily stumble toward the open field, but Sally couldn't move fast enough with Al in tow. Tans grabbed her boot, and Sally fell hard to the ground, stunned at the sudden jolt to her system. She still managed to thrash and scream in desperation as Tans crawled his way toward her face. Hearing the familiar thumping noises of a horse he suddenly jerked up, spotting a rider galloping toward them. He grunted and jumped to his feet. The truck sped off, fishtailing in the grass, the door swinging shut in the dusty trail.

Karen Hollister leaped from her horse and dashed to Sally's side as she still lay stunned on the hot, dirty ground trying to absorb what had just happened. "My God, Sally! Are you all right?" Karen screamed.

Sally grabbed Karen's hand and pulled herself up, slowly leaning on one arm, Al still secured in her bloody grasp. Karen immediately grabbed the lead rope and loosened the grip Sally still had on the calf. She instinctively tied him to a low-hanging mesquite branch and then retrieved a canteen from the saddle of her stammering horse. Karen carefully placed the container up to Sally's lips. "Who was that? Why did he do this to you?" Karen pleaded as she desperately tried to offer water to her helpless friend.

"It was Bill… Bill Tans." Sally managed to stutter but didn't have any other answers for Karen. Sally burst into tears terrifying the young girl enough to grow up and take charge.

"Here, Sally, sit up against this tree and let's get you out of this hot sun. Stay still, and I'll get a blanket from my saddle bag. Chris is supposed to meet me here for a picnic supper after they finished practicing for the rodeo. He'll be here real soon, Sally, I promise." Karen compassionately placed the blanket behind Sally's head as she leaned against the welcome tree trunk.

"Check Al, Karen, please."

Karen rushed to the calf eager to calm Sally. Al had already settled down and was plopped on his side, head perky, eyes serene.

"He's all right, Sally. He's fine!" Karen called in relief.

"Thank God." Sally closed her eyes only to be quickly startled by Karen's adolescent voice.

"Chris is coming! He's almost here!"

Sally breathed a sigh of relief and slumped down on the temporary bedding Karen had placed behind her head. Tears continued to slowly drop from her chin as she quietly thanked God for the rescue.

Karen nervously explained the situation to the young cowboy as he dismounted. Not being a stranger to emergencies, he scoped out Sally and searched the valley with a keen eye. He grabbed Karen by the shoulders and spoke with a calm, commanding voice. "There's no sign of Tans. I'm sure the coward is gone for now. Stay here with Miss McKenna. I can ride faster than you. I'm going to get help. I won't be more than ten minutes. I promise." He then galloped off toward the Hamilton Ranch.

Karen knelt beside Sally. "My God, why did Bill Tans do this to you? What did he want?"

"It's a long story, Karen. You deserve an answer, but—"

"It's okay." The young girl secured Sally's hand in her own and waited.

"Look, my truck is about a mile up the road by the fence. Tans bragged that he did something to it so it wouldn't run. He also smashed the phone. Someone is going to have to come and get it later…" Sally rubbed her eyes, the usual soothing sounds of the birds and insects blaring through her head. The young girl caressed her hand as they both anxiously waited for help to arrive.

Soon flying dust and an engine elevated the already piercing sounds searing Sally's ears. Adam dashed toward her and immediately crumpled to his knees at her side.

"It was Bill Tans," Sally said instantly. "He disabled the truck. It's about a mile back." Adam cursed under his breath. He observed the large lump on her forehead turning blue. *A good sign,* he assessed mentally.

Sally's thoughts were swimming in her head as Adam escorted her to the truck. He spoke decisively. "Karen, tie Al to your horse and walk him slowly back to the ranch. Do you know what to do?"

"Of course. Do you want me to call the outside vet, Dr. Lopez?"

Adam looked at Sally's anguished face. "Naw. Al's fine. You and Chris did okay today. I'm proud of both of you. I left him at the ranch supervising a delivery I was taking care of."

Karen tied Al to her saddle and grabbed the horse's lead rope to begin the journey back to the Straight S. She turned back. "Don't worry. I'll feed Al and I'll have the vet tech look him over just in case." The young girl paused, staring through the window of the truck. "She's going to be all right, isn't she?"

Adam gave her a silent nod before he started up the engine.

"Please, just take me home. I've had worse bumps being thrown from a horse."

Adam's silence seemed an eternity to Sally before he spoke. "Let's just get an X-ray to be sure."

"I know what you're thinking. He didn't rape me. He didn't even try."

Adam tightened his grip on the steering wheel. "I really thought I had taken care of this. If I had even one, small inkling that he was going to do something like this, he wouldn't have left your father's house that night, I swear. I let you down, Sally. Never again."

"Adam, let the law handle this."

"I am the law, remember?"

Sally smiled for the first time, and Adam felt permission to place his hand affectionately on her leg. "You're the peaceful law. You help make rules, not enforce them. Don't do something we'll both regret. You didn't let me down. All of this is the result of booze and greed."

"It's not your worry anymore. We're going to the hospital and getting an X-ray taken." Adam and Sally raced passed the slowing windmills, the weed-clad fences, and the craggy hills.

John arrived at the hospital almost immediately after Adam checked Sally in. Because she had a slight concussion, the doctor recommended Sally stay overnight for observation.

Although vacated from her work and world, the Straight S haunted her thoughts. It was impossible to sleep or relax and, at 6:00 a.m., she phoned home to make sure someone was coming for her right away. There was no answer. After the doctor's visit, she received a quick release, feeling as though she would explode if she remained still a minute longer. Luckily, a nurse from the hospital, an old girlfriend from high school, offered her a ride to the edge of the Hamilton Ranch. Without hesitation, Sally dressed and waited at the nurse's station.

Sally felt an instant relief as she stepped out of the car. She breathed in the air and greedily absorbed all the countryside had to offer. This was familiar territory now, and Sally decided to sort out her thoughts as she walked toward Adam's home at her own pace, reclaiming the land Tans had invaded yesterday.

CHAPTER FIVE

Your wheels are stopped at height of day.
Abandoned work is clear.
The ranch is waiting for your sounds
To prove your work sincere.

You always turn; you do your job.
Windmills creak and groan.
Water cannot clear the earth.
Green will die what farmers sow.

At last we hear you in the sky.
We see your moving flow.
What kept you from your duties?
We missed your morning show.

Shock and horror could only describe what Sally felt when she finally arrived at Adam's house and found her father and Aunt Lucille sitting on the porch drinking coffee and laughing. To her utter surprise and amazement Sally focused in on the fact they were tenderly holding hands while executing their conversation.

Aunt Lucille spotted Sally first and stood up quickly. She walked toward Sally and, with a warm embrace, expressed greetings of joy at seeing her and concern over what had happened the day before.

Sally's father remained seated. When Adam walked out the front door and spotted Sally, he swore under his breath. "What are you doing here? Who brought you from the hospital? Did the doctor release you?"

Still in shock over discovering her father and aunt together, Sally did not comprehend or care to answer any questions Adam shot at her. "Sally, who gave you a ride from the hospital? Why did you leave before I came to get you?" Accepting the situation, he swept her into the house out of the sun. Sally slumped on the couch while Adam pushed aside the sweaty hair from her cheek.

"Were you released this morning? Are you okay?"

"Yes," Sally finally answered, staring directly into his eyes. "How long has my aunt been here?"

Adam looked out the front window. "Several weeks. John and Lucille asked me not to mention it to you. They were planning on telling you—"

"When it was convenient for them?"

"I know this is a shock to you."

"Oh, do you? Do you know this is a shock? Is this experience talking?"

"Sarcasm isn't the answer."

"It really all makes sense now—Dad not coming home for lunch, being tired all the time, his mood swings…" Sally closed her eyes, wishing all of this would just go away.

"Sally, how did you get here?"

"Janna Phillips gave me a ride to the edge of your ranch. I needed time to think and relax."

"I'm sure your father is anxious to talk to you. I'm going to go get him." Adam escaped the room as Sally stared out of the window at the windmills slowly beginning to turn from the steady, summer breeze. The sun was beginning its journey in the blue sky, its destination to top the Hamilton Ranch.

John cautiously entered the room alone. He held his dusty hat, tapping his pant leg before he sat in a chair beside the couch. "Adam told me you were okay. I guess you have a lot of questions. You're entitled to know the whole truth, a truth I should have told you a long time ago. I guess I didn't have the courage."

"I guess it's easy to find courage when you're forced to come up with an explanation." Sally continued to stare out the window.

John ignored her remark. "Sally, your Aunt Lucille and I have been in love for a long time."

"Even when you were married to Mom?"

"Yes."

Sally closed her eyes and faced her father. "Did your interest in Aunt Lucille begin when Mom began to lose her mind?"

"No! It was nothing like that at all. The story is familiar, long, and old…" John's words trailed off as he stood up and gazed out the same window Sally had abandoned.

"Is that your answer to everything, Dad? To look out and stare at land that's not even yours? Are you ever going to be completely honest with me about anything?"

Aunt Lucille walked in with some letters in her hand.

John turned. "No, Lucille, don't. Not yet."

"It's time, John."

"Time for what?" Sally demanded. "For God's sake, someone tell me something."

Sally stared at the letters in Aunt Lucille's hands and responded in confusion. "Those are my letters. I had them the night I went to see Mrs. Wright. I thought the wind had blown them away." Sally thought hard. "I was late feeding Al, so I flung my purse on the corral gate and when I went to see Mrs. Wright they weren't there. You took them?"

"No, I did," John spoke up. "I took the computer sheet and the letters."

"Why?"

John looked to Lucille.

"Because he was protecting me," Lucille said. "He was protecting me because Mrs. Wright and your mother were good friends and he was afraid she'd tell you that your mother was incapable of even writing those last few years. I wrote them. I wrote all of them."

"But they described the land here so perfectly. I could tell she was looking directly at the windmills and hills while she was writing. I painted those windmills. I painted those windmills out there." Sally pointed toward the open prairie.

"They were described from memory…when I was a young girl growing up."

"I don't believe you. You're a liar."

"Sally!" John's voice was cruel and harsh.

"No, John. Let her speak."

Sally felt as though her heart would burst through her chest. "Those letters described major parts of Adam's ranch. How could you have childhood memories of a place that you didn't live on?" There was no response. "All right then, why did you write those letters to me and pretend they were from my mother?" Lucille broke down and cried.

"That's enough." John embraced the sobbing woman. "Lucille wanted to protect you from the fact that your mother was mentally ill. She wanted to get you through college, and she was afraid you would quit school and come home if you knew the truth."

Sally was unsure of his response. "Is that why there were so many excuses for me not to visit?"

"Yes. I took your mother out of town a lot, and that's when Adam began helping me out."

Sally shot Adam a glare, knowing once again she'd been betrayed. She could not bear to hear any more "truths" now that she officially knew he had indeed contributed even more to the conspiracy. "I don't want to hear any more 'long, familiar, or old' stories. What you do is your own business now. You can't possibly think for a minute I believe you were protecting me from my own mother. It's so obvious that you're still keeping the truth from me. And even though I've been begging for answers from you, Dad, I know I'll never get the truth until I go out and find it myself. For God's sake, I was attacked and I don't even know why. How do you live with that?" Sally sighed and stared at her dad and aunt holding each other. "You can both come home for lunch and dinner now. At least I know it wasn't me who kept you away."

"Sally, I didn't know that's what you were thinking," John said sadly.

"Yes, well, if you would have just asked. Please allow me some dignity and leave." Sally closed her eyes until John and Lucille left.

Her father and Aunt Lucille in love—it was difficult almost impossible to comprehend and unbearable to accept.

Adam eventually entered the room and spoke immediately. "Are you all right?" He handed her some cool water, a small, insignificant peace offering. Sally stared at the droplets on the outside of the glass, triggering her memory. "Aunt Lucille was at your house that first day I came to your ranch. It was her glass sitting on the table along with my dad's."

Adam ignored her remark. "She's leaving. She'll be moving—"

"To the Straight S of course."

"They're adults."

"Of course they are. I presume my father stole the computer handout along with the letters to slow down my process of leaving the Straight S. Ironic, isn't it? It's actually spurred my decision to leave right away. They are moving in together, and I am moving out alone." Sally slammed the glass down on the coffee table. "Why couldn't you have been honest with me? Of all the people I wanted to trust and love… Now I have no one. All I wanted from you was the truth. I didn't ask anything else. I didn't expect anything else."

"But I gave you much more."

"Out of guilt? Was that it?" Sally waited for an answer but received none. "I knew it all along. My father sent you over to Benning that day. He knew of my restlessness and curiosity. You were supposed to 'distract' me, weren't you, from my aunt's arrival and my intuition that something wasn't right? He was then free to spend the whole day with her. Congratulations, you did a great job."

"What is between us is real. There was no pretense on my part. I've been a part of your life for a long time. I care for you."

"I am supposed to believe you after all of this?" Sally rubbed her head. "I'm so tired, mentally and physically."

"Sally, you can't move out. You have no place to go."

"I have fifty acres of land, an old house, and a barn," she declared with tenacity.

"That place is not livable yet. It may never be. It's nothing more than a hundred-year-old rundown house. There's no water."

"It's more than most start out with. I still plan to work at the Straight S because I have commitments that I will honor. But for the life of me I won't sleep there anymore. I'll bring my own water and make do at the ranch before I return to my new home every night."

"This is too stupid to even talk about. There are snakes, coyotes—"

"You think so? At least I know what I'm up against out there, and I'm not afraid. I can see my enemy coming."

"You can't live out there alone."

"I can and I will." Sally grabbed Adam's arm. "Tans told me my father murdered Wright. He said the reason he received more money than the others was because he confronted my father with the fact that he was a murderer and my dad had to buy his silence."

"You can't honestly tell me you take one word he says seriously."

"No, I don't believe my father is a murderer. But there is more to Tans than meets the eye, and still something not right about the land, my aunt…information no one will reveal to me. Not only is it frustrating, it hurts. You were once my ally. My whole life you were my ally, and now—"

"Sally…"

"You don't have to say anything. There's nothing that can take away the fact you kept secrets from me when you knew I desperately wanted—needed—some answers. You lied to me." Sally stared at him. "Where is Bill Tans?"

"We're still looking for him."

"He's out there somewhere?"

"Now you know why you shouldn't have walked here alone and why you can't live in that pathetic shack you call a house. He's out there somewhere, and you're making it easy for him."

"It's time I took charge of my life. It will feel good to finally be on my own."

When Adam left, Sally again captured the view from Adam's window. The windmills suddenly stopped turning, the blades resting, and the ominous metal creaking dissipating into silence. The late morning heat was beginning to dominate the skies, squelching the existence of a cool breeze. Sally watched as Adam headed toward the pasture. She felt as though she could curl up and die.

CHAPTER SIX

Metal grids will invade the sky
As machines will lift its load.
A windmill new and eager
Is coming down the road.

Men in force will join with cranes
To secure the manmade force,
A new addition to the farm,
A brand new water source.

Fish will swim, and plants will thrive.
Because the windmills turn,
All the farm is kept alive
As wheels begin to churn.

Sally ceremoniously fed Al that afternoon. Her duties had been
secured by Karen while she recovered from her ordeal with Tans. The
little calf flourished amid the love and attention of all who surrounded
him. Sally's spirits soared for the first time since she discovered the
truth about her father and aunt; maybe because deciding to move out
was the right thing to do despite everyone's protests. Whatever the
reason, Sally basked in her pleasant mood. She tumbled around with
a playful Al when Adam dropped in for his usual check-in.

"How are you going to do his night feeding if you're not here?"

Adam obliterated Sally's cheerful mood. She had already begun to think about his question the minute she had made her decision to move out. "I have an excellent cow barn with some great holding pens right by the house on my land. Why can't I take him with me until he doesn't need night feedings anymore?"

"What about coyotes? You know they're looking for water now. They'll come as close as need be until the fall rains begin. This animal—"

"Spare me the lecture. I'll just drive back until I don't have to anymore. If that's what it takes, I'm willing to do it."

"Okay." Adam petted Al and left.

Aunt Lucille stepped into the pen just as Sally was finishing up gathering the milky buckets and bottles. "You work very hard around here—all those invoices and schedules, feeding the animals." Her aunt leaned against the corral. "I wish you wouldn't leave. We could have those great talks again."

Sally sighed and dropped the buckets. "Come on, Aunt Lucille, let's go sit on the porch for a while." Both women rested in the awkward wooden chairs, an obvious strained silence present as Sally mentally gathered her thoughts. "Aunt Lucille, you and Dad are adults. I don't have any desire to interfere with your relationship. I don't even have the right. If you want to live together or get married or take a trip around the world, it's not for me to say." Sally paused a moment. "I loved my mother, and my only concern now is that she wasn't hurt by all of this."

"Sally, no."

"My point is you have your lives to lead and I have mine. You two chose each other, and I am choosing to move out. I don't have a say in your decision, and quite frankly you don't have a say in mine. I want to move out. I've wanted to move out for a long time and have something to call all my own. I don't care the price I have to pay. Anyway, it just really works out best for everyone."

Aunt Lucille surrendered. "I'm going to miss you."

Sally stood up. "Can I ask you a question?"

"Sure."

"Why did you stay at Adam's house and not come here right away and tell me the truth? Why did you have to involve him?"

Aunt Lucille's silence spoke volumes.

"Never mind. I didn't really think I'd get an answer anyway." Sally left to retrieve the abandoned buckets as her aunt covered her face.

That evening Sally stuffed her bag with essential paraphernalia, showered for an extensive period of time, filled a five-gallon water jug with fresh water, haphazardly folded up a sleeping bag, and absconded with some food supplies from the pantry. She loaded the truck herself with everything but her duffel bag. Unfortunately, the realization of having to sleep in the back of an old farm vehicle until at least one room in the old house could be cleaned and fixed to be animal free was foremost in her mind. Her alarm clock would prove essential for knowing when to feed Al through the night for the next eight weeks. Of course, she didn't even know when Al would join her, but whether he was with her or on the ranch she would still feed him and care for him. As Sally was packing a last-minute bag, her father knocked on her door and walked in. He had barely spoken to her that day, and in her heart Sally knew he probably wasn't able to find the words to comfort her or force her to understand how he felt inside.

"Sally, wait a while before you go. Let a few of the boys go over and fix up that house first, and then you can move in."

"Daddy, I appreciate that, but I don't want to wait. Adam has finished fixing all the fences for me, and, quite frankly, I feel the need to be somewhere safe."

"Safe? Safe out there alone?"

"Dad..."

"Well, I suppose you just have to have your way. Your mother was exactly the same." John shook his head and left.

Sally was eternally thankful her father couldn't read her mind. She was elated and petrified to be on her own, especially now. She was afraid of Bill Tans. She was afraid of failure. She was afraid to be alone.

Another knock interrupted her paradox of thoughts. Aunt Lucille stood at the door, dirty from working in the garden all day. She looked tired but unusually happy.

"Come on in. I'm just finishing up. You shouldn't work all day in the heat... Well, I guess you know what you're doing. You grew up in the country with all the windmills."

"I can't apologize to you, Sally, for being in love with your father..." Lucille left the room as unobtrusively as she entered.

"I didn't ask you to, Aunt Lucille," Sally quietly said to an empty doorway and then ceremoniously picked up her essentials and abandoned the house. She tossed her duffel bag in the back of the truck and yelled that she'd be back to feed Al to her dad and aunt, who were standing on the porch, hands intertwined.

Sally drove up to the locked gate and immediately opened the creaking metal guard. Lord Johnson and Lady Grace were grazing around the small stock tank near the road, their tails swishing. Sally pulled up beside the crumbling porch steps of the protruding, antique house. She smiled. It was all hers, and she loved it even as awful as it looked now. Sally quickly yet carefully cleared away some of the grasses by the broken building to start a fire before the setting sun stole her advantage. She scoped out a good spot to practice for the Abilene rodeo scheduled for the end of August. Lady Grace was great at barrel racing even though Sally knew that now the horse would be practically impossible at handling sedate chores. Barrel racing heated a horse's blood, which never cooled. Lord Johnson, on the other hand, was a quiet, calm gelding, and she knew she would use him for the everyday ranch work. The exhilaration Sally felt was inexplicable. She'd put unbelievable burdens on herself, yet she couldn't be happier.

Having already eaten and showered at the Straight S, Sally felt that welcome sense of peace and contentment as she lay in the back of the pickup on her sleeping roll, her head propped on her saddle. She stared up at the darkening, cloudy sky and breathed in the unique smell of the pastures drifting off to sleep until invasive noises alerted her calmed senses.

Sally instinctively placed her hand on a rifle, reacting to the sound of an engine but relaxed when she recognized Adam's truck. She watched him pull in past the gate and drive up to the house.

Adam anticipated her question. "I bought the locks for the gate when we were fixing the fences, remember? I still had one of the keys."

"You brought Al!" Sally screeched as she spotted the animal in the back of the truck. She jumped up, hugged the small calf, and kissed his nose. In the cab of the truck, the Blue Heeler pup suddenly stuck his head out of the open window, barked, and wagged his tail. Sally snatched him up and lovingly rubbed his fur.

"I couldn't see you up all night going back and forth, from here to the Straight S. I checked out your holding pens. They are in good condition. Besides, if there's any trouble there will be two of us around to thwart any enemies."

"You are staying the night?"

"Yes."

"So you do understand why I have to be here?"

"I suppose." Adam took out a tarp and set it up. Sally secured Al in a nearby corral, and afterward both relaxed around the fire drinking coffee, the Heeler curled up beside Adam's boot.

Sally stared at the pup. "That dog has already taken to you." The flames were bright, and the mesquite logs popped and sputtered, protesting their consumption. "You should be at your own ranch, Adam. You and I both know that. I do have a gun."

"You're right. I should be home." Adam threw some twigs on the fire, the crackling noise adding to the symphony of sounds emanating from the flames. "I figured I owed you one. Look, I did your dad a favor. He's like a father to me and a true friend. I hated being dishonest with you. I hope you believe that. At the time I thought I was protecting you and helping out someone whom I trusted and respected very much, and still do."

"It still hurts to be lied to, no matter what the motive is, and it's still wrong."

"I understand."

"How can we be friends without trust?"

"Trust is a funny thing. Sometimes people think it's doing what you expect of another person."

"That's not true in this case."

Adam drank his coffee methodically. "I owed you one. I know that. So let's work together and not against each other."

"You really want to work together this time—dare I say it once again—like partners? True to the definition of the word?" Sally asked skeptically.

"I kind of like the idea."

"I still haven't officially given you a piece of my mind for lying to me. And I still don't know if I believe anything you have to say. As a matter of fact, I may never be able to believe anything you tell me again."

"That's a pity, considering I hold the key to answering all those questions you have."

"What do you mean?"

"Are you changing your mind?"

"I don't know. What do you mean?"

"Are you trusting me now because you expect something of me?"

Sally stood to give herself an advantage. "You're trying to turn all of this around and blame me for all this dishonesty, and I won't let you do that."

"Sally, sit, please. There's something you need to know. Mrs. Wright left town yesterday. She moved to Arizona to live with her sister."

"What about her real estate office? What about her real estate partner?"

"She closed down the office. Her partner had already moved away several months ago."

"But why would she leave? This was her home."

"It's a term we use kind of loosely around here, isn't it? I guess she didn't feel like it was her home anymore. You asked her a few questions, and then she must have felt compelled to leave town."

"But she seemed so happy just weeks ago. She sold me my land. I don't understand. Did she tell anyone good-bye or say anything?"

"I have no idea. But I think you can see now the importance of straightening out our agreement about working together."

"Yes, I do, but—"

"So you don't want my help? You're so intelligent and capable. I can't believe you would pass up this opportunity. You once asked me how much power I have. Remember, I have a foothold here in this part of Texas and a lot of people help support it. I know a lot of facts about a lot of people. Do you understand the implication of what I am saying? Quite frankly, I could take your land away with a snap of my fingers."

"But this is my land. No one can take that away from me unless I didn't finish paying for it."

"Interesting words. Are you talking money?"

"Of course. What are you talking about?"

"I'm talking about paying dues, the kind that give you real power and real respect."

"You, as my friend, would take away what I have a legal right to?"

"If it meant saving you from self-destruction."

"You see why it is difficult to agree to work together when you sound so ominous all the time? What do you mean?"

"You need to trust me. There's a killer on the loose now—"

"A killer?" Sally, taken aback, rubbed the newly formed goose-bumps on her arms.

"Seems Tans had a bar fight in Benning last night with some seedy character and stabbed him to death. So you see, Sally, he's got nothing to lose by coming back here to settle an old score."

"Bill Tans? You're scaring me."

"I hope so. So, what about being partners? It was your idea to begin with."

"All right. Why not? I'm not exactly striking up points alone. But I still have issues with the trust thing."

Adam threw his sleeping bag next to Sally's and spoke apologetically for his previous words. "I didn't want you to know about Tans, but you didn't give me a choice. I would never have intentionally frightened you if—"

"If it wasn't necessary to get what you want?"

"Well done. But I do know a little more than you do about surviving and succeeding in Texas. But, on the other hand, in all honesty, if it wasn't for you, that calf over there would probably be dead. History would not be in the making as we speak. Many calves before Al died by our mixed breeding and experimentation, millions of dollars spent. He could have easily been another casualty, but, Sally, you saved him. I don't have your instincts with animals. Personally, I don't have a problem about admitting I don't know everything."

"Sure you don't." Sally sighed heavily. "Give me a break."

Adam sighed. "I'm tired." He climbed into his sleeping roll.

"We're not sleeping next to each other."

Adam smiled and turned away from her. "Your scruples emerge at the most convenient times. Don't worry. I can control myself. What about you? Should I sleep with one eye open?"

Sally relaxed, grateful for the humor. She unrolled the sleeping bag and looked at her watch. "I have Al's food in these ice chests. He doesn't have to be fed for an hour. I had better reset the alarm."

"Do me a favor, Sally. Don't stay up with him. Your dad said you're going to be in Benning all day tomorrow. Hollister and your Aunt Lucille are going with you. You'll need all your energy and wits about you."

"I don't want to be with my aunt right now. I don't want to say anything I might regret. I haven't had a chance to think this whole situation through."

"Think fast because she's going. She can go with you to places that Hollister cannot go. Do you get my drift?"

"Because of this so-called partner-trust thing, do I have a choice?"

"It's your decision. If you want my help, you have to be alive…"

"True. And if I am going to milk you for information I can't make waves…"

"A pragmatist to the end. Now, speaking of pragmatics, I am going to sleep."

"Well, obviously you don't have any problem controlling yourself." Sally smiled and again sought the serenity of the night sky. The stars remained stationary as the clouds danced through their flickering bodies.

"By the way, I'm leaving for Austin tomorrow. I've got work that needs to be done before we meet in special session next month. I'm behind and I don't like it. I won't be here for a while."

"Sure. You have to answer when Austin calls." Sally slept for an hour, and when she awoke at 10:00 p.m., Adam was asleep a gun lay by his side. She knew instinctively that the slightest irregularity would awaken him. Feeding Al was not an irregularity. Sally again greedily inhaled the smell of her land as it slept and cooled the grasses and trees in anticipation of the next day's heat. The energy provided by the Texas night was exhilarating. Sally fed Al at 10:00 p.m. and at 2:00 a.m. There was a difference now in the way she felt when she fed the young calf. It was as though owning land allowed her membership into an exclusive club that exuded her confidence and strength.

Sally awoke to the smell of fresh coffee at 5:00 a.m. Adam had already eaten breakfast and was loading up Al in the back of the pickup. She spotted some fried ham and eggs on a tin plate and, requisitioning a dirty towel, bent over to retrieve them off the grill of the open fire. She tossed a bit of food to the pup who immediately quit following Adam after spotting Sally's movements. "Thanks for the breakfast!"

Adam slammed the tailgate shut. "It's your turn next. Hurry up, we've got to clean up here before you leave, and don't give that dog scraps! We have to drop the pup off at my ranch before we go to the Straight S."

Adam and Sally picked up Hollister and Aunt Lucille at the Straight S about 6:00 a.m. and they all drove to Benning, even Al. Adam left immediately for Austin, and a pang of sadness overtook Sally as she remembered four weeks earlier when he had approached her in this field and asked her to share old memories. Could it be possible for a lifetime to pass in only a month's time?

Aunt Lucille sat beside Sally among the grasses in the open lot after everyone was set and up and ready for the first customers. "Your father will have to be the one to tell you the things about his past." She paused. "I thought I could come here and do it for him, but I can see that's impossible."

"Is that why you came today Aunt Lucille?" Sally rose, dusted off her jeans, and jumped onto the back of the truck. "You could tell me if you wanted." Sally's legs dangled from the tailgate.

"Yes, I suppose, but I wouldn't be able to answer your questions. Your dad has the reasons buried. They are not my motives or part of my explanation."

"Come on, Aunt Lucille, all I want is the truth. Motives don't interest me." Sally stared ahead.

"But that's the whole point. You won't understand unless you know why we did—"

"We?" Sally stressed sarcastically. "This has been in the works for a long time, hasn't it?" She looked at Aunt Lucille's hurt face and felt a pang of guilt. She loved her aunt. Nothing could strip that love away. "I'm sorry for everything that has happened. I wished I felt differently about things. Perhaps when I understand, perhaps when everyone around here will finally share all their secrets." Sally looked at her watch. "I have to feed Al. He didn't eat that much this morning after we arrived. I guess it was the ride and I tried to feed him right away." She jumped down from the tailgate and retrieved the bottles from the ice chest.

Sally happened to look up at the precise moment Dr. Lopez's mobile veterinary truck cruised by. She waved good-naturedly, and when he spotted her, Dr. Lopez uncharacteristically jerked his truck into the field. Sally and Lucille walked up to the bright red vehicle and leaned against the door.

"Hello, Dr. Lopez. I suppose everything is okay in your life." Sally smiled, remembering his familiar words.

"Hello Sally. I am happy that you waved to me. I was looking for a familiar face in the crowd. I am very frustrated right now. It seems I need some help in finding a real estate office that is for sale." He fumbled through some papers on the messy seat.

"Do you mean the one Mrs. Wright has for sale? News travels fast," Sally responded, surprised.

"I have been looking for a permanent building to set up my veterinary practice for some time," he said, sitting in the truck, engine running. "Mrs. Wright called me before she left town and suggested I look at it. She told me I could have it…oh, yes, lock, stock and barrel she said. Between you and me, I think she left in a hurry. Can you believe it, she said the key is under the mat?! Just like the movies, right? I have an idea where it is, but she spoke so fast, and sometimes I hear more in Spanish than in English!"

"Being from around here, I would have thought you of all people would be familiar with all the buildings. It's on FM 104 near Carley's old place," Sally offered.

"Oh, I understand now, it is the same building where Mr. Wright used to have his office set up. That is all she had to say to me."

"Mr. Wright had an office set up outside of his ranch?" Sally's instincts were once again aroused, hearing information pertinent to her dilemma. "Wasn't he just a rancher?"

"Sure he was—the second half of his life. Didn't you know the Wrights moved down from the north when he retired from being a lawyer full time? You of all people should have known that," Dr. Lopez teased.

"I deserved that, but what brought him down here?"

"What he told everyone was he hated the fast pace living in the frozen hell of the north. He did a little bit of local stuff, but basically enjoyed doing ranch work."

Something clicked inside of Sally's head. "What kind of local stuff did he do down here?"

"I think he did legal papers for surveys in the county."

Aunt Lucille looked up at Sally. "Did you know Mr. Wright was a lawyer?" Sally asked her aunt.

"Everybody did, I guess, although I'm not quite sure. You know if you haven't lived here for at least thirty years you are still an outsider. Remember, I haven't been in Texas for over twenty years. Does it make a difference?" Aunt Lucille asked, a little too quietly.

"Aunt Lucille, you know it does." Sally turned toward Dr. Lopez. "Thank you very much. You'll never know how much you've helped me."

"Okay. I don't know what I did, but I am glad to help and thank you very kindly for the directions," Dr. Lopez said politely as he drove off toward the Farm Road. Sally shuffled back to the truck, plopping herself down on the tailgate. She hit the metal hard with her fist. "Now I know how Mr. Wright found out about my dad's name on those deeds."

Al's bawling for food jerked Sally into reality. She leaped from the truck and kicked through the high grasses until she reached the ice chest where she had propped up the bottles. Aunt Lucille followed. "Deeds are a matter of public record," she told Sally.

"Of course they are, Aunt Lucille, but no one notices the ordinary. Don't you see? You pass the same things every day and never notice the extraordinary unless you have a reason. Mr. Wright worked on those surveys and was forced to scrutinize the books. No one else cares about county deeds unless they have a specific reason. But it was his job to really look. The clerk in Addison already told me that the county came in and did some survey work and changed the names and numbers of some roads they were going to take over. They had to hire a lawyer to take care of the legalities. He said they started about five years ago. Mr. Wright was that lawyer and he found out something that my father didn't like. He found out that my father's name was on the deed to the Straight S Ranch and somehow that fact would change a lot of people's lives."

"Your father already told you why he had to change the names on those papers and that's why Tans and the others received money."

"Oh, come on, Aunt Lucille. Why was my father's name on the deed to begin with? And do you think for one minute I believe my father would pay off a lowlife like Tans so people wouldn't get the wrong idea about him? My father would never be intimidated enough to let someone blackmail him. I've lived with him all my life. He may have convinced Adam but not me. I knew from the start there was another reason, and now Dr. Lopez has given me the opportunity I've been looking for all along." Sally fed Al his bottle and looked up at Aunt Lucille. "But of course you probably already know what I'm trying to find out. That's okay. You don't have to answer," she said smugly.

Evening rolled around and still no sign or word from Adam. The band warmed up with the usual testing of the mikes, the haphazard drum beats, and strumming of guitars. All Sally could do at this point was to stare down Main Street, hoping to spot Adam's truck zooming down the road. Her patience was wearing thin, and she began to snap at the people around her. Aunt Lucille had pretty much distanced herself from Sally except for the time they ate lunch and cleaned up a bit in midafternoon. They did enjoy a pleasant conversation while they consumed chicken sandwiches and onion rings in the cool air of the local cafe, and Sally derived some joy observing Aunt Lucille as she reacquainted herself to almost everyone who had come out for the sale. She also walked the perimeter of the field with the ranch hands and eagerly entertained the youngest members of the crowd. Sally savored the old Aunt Lucille, not the new one she had recently molded in her mind.

Sally had the foresight to purchase sandwiches for supper from the restaurant in case she was needed at the dance. Al was already fed and a diverse number of people purposefully came to observe him and question Sally about his less-than-humble beginnings. She felt a sense of pride responding to the strangers and spoke knowledgeably about the new herd she hoped he would one day produce. The tack sale attracted numerous country people as well as city people that day. Al retained star status. Even the newspaper reporters attended the monthly gathering to view and record the possible creation of a new breed of cattle. As evening descended upon the crowd all the outsiders left, abandoning the Straight S family.

Sally, clad in her blue jeans and casual shirt, surveyed the lot, her hair blowing in the welcome breeze. She finally began to enjoy the evening, her worries dissipating with the sweltering sun. Sally smiled as she noticed Karen and Chris holding hands, laughing as they traipsed through the field among the leftover goods. Another endless batch of puppies entangled themselves in their temporary home and hay stacks reached high in the air, while children played King of the Mountain, knocking down the squares of bound grass. Rabbits, hamsters, chicks, and many other kinds of dispensable small animals chased their fellow inmates in the wire cages. Sally smiled. This could have been a month ago.

"Hello, beautiful. Don't I know you?"

Sally breathed a sigh of relief as she faced Adam and instinctively gave him a lingering hug. She embraced a feeling of security and a link to a familiar past.

"Hey," Adam said softly, "are you all right? Did something happen today?" There was caution and alarm in his voice, an innate alarm synonymous to a rancher who constantly senses the perils of Mother Nature.

Sally released her hold. "No, nothing happened. I just missed your ominous presence. Well, almost nothing happened. I did find something out from Dr. Lopez that I think warrants further investigation." She looked into Adam's sullen eyes and suddenly felt guilty. "You look so tired. Do you want something to eat? I have some sandwiches."

"Why don't we head over to the Benning Café? You can tell me your news, and I can tell you mine."

"Sounds like a fine idea."

As Sally and Adam passed the burger place that had been the sight of their first date, a thought entered her mind. "Adam, that day we were eating here, it was Sam Reel who came up to the truck, wasn't it? It was him you were arguing with. What did he want that day?"

"He was telling me that Tans was at my house and had seen your aunt Lucille. Tans thought he deserved some kind of extra compensation for this knowledge. My foreman, Sam, was supposed to keep an eye on him. He obviously bungled the job. I went back to the ranch to check on Lucille. I walked out of the house to find you in the strangest mood. I have to admit I would have rather faced a tornado that day than your temper." Adam paused. "But, it helps to be a representative in the state capitol, and I think we actually have some real connections, which may help us both."

Sally was relieved to know Adam finally believed in her, even though she couldn't help but still feel a bit suspicious about him. This situation was something she had no control over right now, and Sally was beginning to respect things in her life that were out of control. She had lived in Texas too long not to know the foreboding that coincided with country life. "Adam, what exactly did my father tell you about my aunt Lucille before she arrived?"

Adam sighed and stretched, leaving one hand on the steering wheel. "Your father confided in me about your aunt, his reservations…He was waiting for the right time to bring Lucille out here. For three months at a distance, I watched you pouring your soul out over the land. It brought back the memories of a young girl. I had been available for you in the past, but it was easy back then. It was not so easy now. I knew things I couldn't tell you; I had secrets to keep from you. I couldn't face you until your father asked me to come into town to be with you while Lucille arrived. I guess it was the excuse I needed." Adam stopped the truck and turned toward Sally. "I can't find the words to reach you, Sally, like in the past. I looked after you back then, my duty like a brother, but everything is different now. You are a woman, independent, motivated, stubborn. Trust me, I don't feel like the brother now." He leaned closer to Sally and kissed her gently. She said nothing until Adam's hug was almost unbearable. "I'm sorry." Sally knew it was an apology that stretched far beyond an almost unbearable embrace.

Sitting at the table in the café, Sally could barely contain herself as the waitress repeated their order numerous times before leaving the table. Sally's verbal announcement was immediate. "Did you know that Mr. Wright was a lawyer before he came down here and that he did the legal work for the county when they surveyed the roads and land? And did you know that this was done five years ago, about the time I left Texas?"

Adam sighed. "Wright's signature was all over the record books when I checked into them. I didn't know the extent of his involvement, and, since you were so intent on questioning Mrs. Wright, I was afraid you might accidentally say something about the deeds to her while y'all were conducting business. Don't go crazy on me. That was the only information I kept from you about those books, and I was planning on telling you when I got back, especially after what I learned in Austin today."

"If we're going to get to the bottom of this, then we'd better not hold any of our past indiscretions against each other. What has been your hesitation about all of this? From the beginning you have acted as though you have had a personal stake in what I'm trying to find out. That is the part I really don't understand."

"I don't think you can understand. How can I expect you to empathize what my life has been up to now? To feel the last eighteen years of what I've been accomplishing? You were right; getting this 23rd District redistricted wasn't easy. Actually, that's like saying a late summer breeze is as powerful as a tornado. I was forced to fight anyone and everyone every second of every single day to establish new boundaries, and for the best reason in the world. Trust me, a day didn't go by in Austin that I wasn't sparring in the ring trying to gain power or get the control we needed to do business out here in a place most people don't even know exists. And yet laws were constantly being made every day by these same lawmakers and we, the people who actually lived here, had to abide by them, the subsidy law to name one example. It was as though we didn't have any say about our own lives."

"Our situations are not unfamiliar to each other."

Adam pushed his plate aside. "Originally, the people who settled Texas were under no scrutiny. They were free to fight and deal however they chose to get what they wanted, what they needed. We were still a frontier even at the turn of the twentieth century. While New York and Boston were enjoying the theater, we were literally fighting for our survival. No one cared if a little bit of shady business went on as long as ranches were being formed and prosperity found its way to Texas and that prosperity was advantageous to the whole country. We were feeding a growing giant. The long anticipated railroads were being built, and if a few toes had to be stepped on then that's just the way it was. Everyone looked at the bottom line—nothing else."

Sally said nothing, wondering if that unspoken rule still existed. She knew in her heart it did.

"The trouble with all of this glorious Texas history is that those of us who are living here now are paying for the sins of the past. Obscure things unexpectedly come back to haunt us one day, and we suddenly have no control over our own lives. I decided I personally couldn't live with that, so I went to Austin and fought for the right to have a say as to what goes on in the parts of Texas I have devoted my life to."

"Adam, is someone trying to take your land away?"

"After being in Austin today, I hate to say it, but it looks as though it might be your dad."

"What? That's impossible! My father—"

"I know. I didn't mean that the way it sounded. It's just that there are some sealed records concerning your dad that only a state judge can open and only under certain conditions. Seems Captain King had more influence and strings to pull than I originally thought, and those strings are just as tight as they were a hundred years ago. These records directly concern your dad and the Straight S and, unfortunately, Hamilton Ranch. That's why I have to find out the truth."

"So now it means as much to you as it does to me."

"I don't want to believe what the paperwork is telling me, and yet I don't have another explanation." Adam sat back in his chair. "I wasn't ignoring your comment. We'll get to the bottom of all of this. I believe the truth begins with Wright's personal records. I know Mrs. Wright must have just locked up her office and taken off. Perhaps they are still in there. But it's been so long since—"

"Adam, do you remember when Mrs. Wright gave me the computer sheet with all the land listings on it? She told me that the computer was her husband's and that she was very proud of the fact she had taken a class to learn how to use it. She said he kept records of everything. I'll bet you he had all of his files on CDs or on the hard drive, maybe even an external hard drive. I'm good with computers. I bet I can break a code to access anything he had in there."

"That's great, if we only had access to the computers…"

"But we do. Dr. Lopez has the key. He came by the lot in Benning today on his way to look over the office. He wants to buy it. He told me Mrs. Wright said he could purchase the building, lock, stock, and barrel. That must mean she left everything, including the computer. I bet he's still over there checking out the place. You know how slow he is!"

Adam glanced at his watch. "I think we still have time to drive on over before everyone heads back to the ranch. This is important, Sally, but I have to make sure Al is taken care of before we go."

Sally understood, and the two hurried out of the restaurant and headed back toward the tack sale. The familiar music was audible from blocks away. Adam pulled into the lot where Al was resting comfortably under a mesquite tree. The vet tech who was attending Al was chewing on a piece of hay, propped up against a tree. "He looks happy enough; actually, both of them do." Sally laughed. Adam turned off the engine and loaded the unresisting, but noisy, animal into the back of the truck and escorted him back to the Straight S. Frustrated by the length of time it took Adam to unload the calf and secure him in the pen, Sally impatiently waited in the truck until they left for the real estate office.

Sensing her mood, Adam squeezed her leg. "First things, first, or this would be for nothing."

When they arrived, Dr. Lopez was still scrutinizing the contents of the building. Adam opened the front door, calling out for a response. He walked into Mrs. Wright's old office and spotted Dr. Lopez sitting on a stool staring at a computer screen. He recognized Adam's voice and called for him to "come on in."

"What are you doing here, Adam?" he asked, still staring at the screen.

"Sally and I wanted to know if we could look through a few of Mr. Wright's old records. It's pretty important, Tony. We think some information we need might still be located on this computer."

Dr. Lopez smiled and stood shaking Adam's hand. "Sure. I was just going over these listings Mrs. Wright had on a CD. Actually, I think I was caught up a bit in the past. Many of these parcels of land used to be owned by some really nice people I knew when I was a kid. It is sad to think these large ranches no longer exist. I believe the Straight S and the Hamilton Ranch will be two of the few surviving ranches in this portion of South Texas." Dr. Lopez shook his head and turned toward Sally and Adam. "I am sure to buy this place, so since it will be mine anyway, you can look over anything you want. For me, I am going home. It has been a long day. Too many animals! When you are finished, please lock the door." Adam shook his hand, and the doctor left.

Sally instantly began searching the permanent hard drive on the computer, while Adam hunted for any CDs that may have been filed away. "I don't see anything here!" Sally yelled loudly, frustrated after an hour of searching. "But of course there may be endless—"

"Hey, I think I've got something!" Adam had wedged himself in a small room, pushing against some loose wood. His efforts revealed a concealed space loaded with shelves. He reached in the hole and pulled out a large, metal box. Adam immediately opened it to examine the contents. "That old dog. I guess being a lawyer he couldn't resist labeling, filing, and keeping records of everything he did. My own legal CDs should be in such order." Sally joined Adam in the storage closet, peering around his chest as he rifled through the metal disks. "There must be a hundred CDs in here," Adam said. "And they were all thoughtfully labeled and dated for us." He smiled. "Come on. We're taking these back to the ranch."

"But, Adam, we have a computer right here. Let's find out what he knew right now."

Adam examined his watch. "No, we have to head back to Benning. But I want to lock these in my safe before we go. They will be there when we get ready to look at them."

"Adam, I'll stay here and you can go back—"

"No!" Adam snapped. "You can't stay here alone. I don't have to remind you about Tans, do I?"

Sally sighed in frustration. "Okay, so what is it we're doing?"

"We'll go to my ranch, drop these off, stop by the Straight S to feed Al, and then head on to Benning to lead everyone back home. Sally, ranch life goes on no matter what else comes up, and, remember, the vet tech doesn't possess the instincts you do."

"I think this partner thing sucks," Sally said as she slammed the door on the truck.

"Think what you want. This is for your safety."

"I think it is for both our safeties."

It was well past midnight before Sally and Adam pulled into the gate of her fifty acres. They both showered; Sally brought some beef and vegetables to cook, and they gathered Al's food for the remainder of the night. If the traveling back and forth bothered him, his appetite and disposition didn't reflect any consequences. Sally knew Al's newfound residency would end if he showed the slightest amount of stress. She mentally anguished at the thought of waking up in only an hour to feed him, but it was an impossibility to confide her feelings to Adam, as she already knew what his response would be. Her pride would not allow her to show weakness at this point. Sally held the wide, metal gate open while Adam drove the truck through the pitted dirt entrance. They both secured Al, and, after setting her alarm, Sally immediately plopped down in the back of the truck. The night was clear, and the insects were as noisy as ever. When Sally awoke to feed Al, Adam was asleep beside her, his arm around her waist. She silently slipped out and jumped off the back of the truck to retrieve the little calf's bottles.

The morning sun rose all too soon, and Sally awoke this time to find Adam gone. Al was obviously fed, as he was quiet, and there was a note under the coffee pot sitting beside the smoking ashes of an earlier fire. She scanned the note quickly and then threw it down in frustration as she kicked the ashes beside her, the note curling in the red embers. A missing truck and hammering noises from the house confirmed what Adam had written. He would return at noon but meanwhile some of the hands from the Hamilton Ranch would be working on the house while he was gone. If Sally needed anything or if Tans unexpectedly dropped by someone would be close to help her. Adam had spoken with her father, and John gave her the morning off from the Straight S.

Sally's anger and confusion kept her productive. The thoughts that her father might have something to do with taking Adam's ranch and the fact that Bill Tans had said her father was a murderer haunted her every moment. There were many chores waiting for her at the Straight S, but she did need to feed Al and there were a few chores to be attended to on her own land. She could also finally practice her barrel racing for the rodeo in Abilene.

Sally stacked fresh wood on the old ashes, reviving the fire, and plopped some meat, potatoes, and carrots in the water of a large kettle. She stirred in gravy by adding some flour and then lifted the heavy, cast iron pot onto a metal grill to cook. She heard the windmills in the distance and hopped in the bed of the truck in time to see the blades beginning to rotate around the wheels. "Something wrong?" someone yelled from the house.

"No!" Sally yelled back. "Just taking a look."

Sally stomped through the high grass to retrieve a saddle, blanket, and other paraphernalia out of the barn. She rounded up a reluctant horse from the field after attaching the lead rope to her halter. It seemed all Lady Grace wanted to do anymore was graze on the tasty grasses abundant in the fields. Both the horses' bellies were growing large, an unfortunate side effect of pasture feeding. Uncharacteristic of Lady Grace, Sally was having a difficult time controlling the horse, but she secured the animal to a cedar post, brushed her down, and placed the saddle blanket across her back before saddling her. Sally wondered if her nervous disposition might be from the new, unfamiliar field, so she decided to ride close to the house and first walked the horse slowly through the pattern she would be using for the barrel race. This would also assure Sally that there were no holes or large rocks the horse could stumble over. Lady Grace calmed a bit, but she was still difficult to lead and mount. After the barrels were in place, with the kind help of one of the hands, Sally repeated her routine. At first, the horse kept knocking over the second barrel on the sharp turn and Sally had to admit that they were both pretty rusty, but after a while the repetition paid off. A few of the hands cheered her on, ensuring an adrenaline rush throughout each ride.

Adam drove up around noon and leaned against his truck, silently admiring Sally's riding, taking pride in her skill. She spotted him after one of her turns and galloped up to the truck. The horse reared back and nearly threw Sally, but she quickly took control and dismounted.

"What's wrong with your horse?" Adam asked, concerned.

"I don't know. She's been skittish all morning," Sally said, out of breath and sweating. "I'll go unsaddle her and brush her down. She's sweating as much as me."

Adam followed the two over to the barn and Sally began brushing Lady Grace.

Anticipating retribution, Adam spoke. "Now don't be mad. You didn't get much sleep last night, so I decided not to wake you. If it will keep you from unleashing that sharp tongue on me, I promise never to be considerate again and let you sleep."

Sally sighed. "Jerk. You didn't get much rest either, after being in Austin all day. Are you hungry? I have a stew cooking over the fire. It should be ready by now."

"Sounds inviting."

Sally removed Lady Grace's halter, and the horse instantly bolted toward the field. Adam and Sally sauntered toward the old house, the grasses rustling beneath their boots. "That was some pretty good riding. Maybe you do have a chance in the rodeo after all."

"My acceptance letter came in the mail. Did I tell you?"

"Congratulations. Don't mind if I come and watch you win, do you?"

"My own private rooting section. What more could I ask for in this lifetime?"

Both leaned against the old, wooden porch steps and consumed their simple cuisine alone as the hands had driven to the ranch to eat their noon meal. Sally swallowed her last morsel and rested the tin plate in her lap. "Tell me, Adam, did you find out anything—"

"Not meaning to interrupt you"—he smiled—"but I think I know what you're going to ask and I've been working all morning on the ranch with some new cattle that just came in. Besides, you're the computer expert around here. When you're finished and the hands come back we'll go over to the house and look at the CDs together."

"I'm done. Riding made me hungry." Sally and Adam left the civilization of the porch steps and lay in the tall grasses waiting for the hands to return while he told her with pride about the new cattle he'd ordered from Montana.

"I'd love to see them." Sally suddenly shot up her eyes settling on Lady Grace. "I wonder why my horse is so spooked today. Look at her out there."

"Could be a lot of different reasons. You know horses; they're like babies. Anything can bother them."

"I suppose. I just have this funny feeling."

Adam pulled Sally next to him. "Why don't you ride her over to the Straight S and have the vet look at her?"

"Yeah, I might."

"Suit yourself." He closed his eyes and basked in human silence and nature clamor. Sally nestled further in the grasses and drifted off, temporarily forgetting Lady Grace.

The returning hammering and noise from the dilapidated building jolted Sally into reality. She slowly rose and brushed the grass from her jeans and shirt. "Adam, you fixed my fences every night until they were finished, and now you're fixing my house. I'll get it done myself eventually, you know. I can't allow this to go on."

Adam yawned and sighed. "You know, Sally, you stay up all night with my calf and work hard all day besides feeding Al. Your whole schedule is centered on that animal over there because we both know the stake he holds in the future of ranching. You most assuredly saved Al from certain demise and have secured a place for him in history by nurturing that fellow to health, and I am not to be 'allowed' to help you in return? That doesn't seem very fair to me." He stood up and slapped his pants with his hat. "I'll take Al back to Hamilton Ranch and turn him over to Chris."

Sally smiled. "Point taken. It just seems so one sided lately."

"I feel the same way."

"You know, you once told me it was my job to take care of Al."

"We'd better be on our way if we are going to decipher those CDs," Adam said quickly.

"We need to load up Al and take him to the ranch with us. Then I can feed him when we take a break. I have a feeling we are going to be staring at a computer for a long time."

"I don't think that calf would go anywhere without you anyway. Would you like to load up the horses?"

"Very funny." Sally glanced up at Lady Grace again, still wondering what could be causing her strange behavior.

Sally's eyes ached as she stared intently at the bright screen while Adam sat close beside her. So far, all they'd discovered was the fact that the county had hired Mr. Wright to draw up the legal papers concerning road name changes. Thousands of entries necessitated careful scrutiny by Sally and Adam. All the entries they'd reviewed had passed inspection. Sally glared at the remaining disks lying on the table beside the computer and sighed. "This is going to take longer than I thought. Maybe I'd better go feed Al."

"Okay," Adam said. "I'm going to head over to the south field but hopefully I'll be right back. Go ahead and start without me if I take too long."

"I'd better call Dad. I didn't get the afternoon off as well. He may need me."

Sally ejected the CD and headed toward the truck to retrieve Al's food. The puppy was nipping on the heels of her boot as she watched Adam speed down the dirt road heading toward one of the south pastures. As Sally was tromping toward the holding pen, an eerie feeling invaded her serenity. The ranch was uncharacteristically silent. She cautiously summed up her surroundings, deducing that all the hands normally around the house must be at her property. She was alone.

CHAPTER SEVEN

I lay among the shadows
Produced by windmills' stance.
I dream about my future.
Success is just a chance.

Some windmills last, yet others fall.
Which will nature shield?
To stand and serve forever
Or lie in earth's great field.

Fallen metal disappears.
Rust quickens its demise.
But if it stands up once again,
It survives among the skies.

"What the hell is going on around here?" Adam yelled once again as he heard Al bawling and banging against the buckets hanging on the fence. The puppy jumped outside the gate, barking at the terrified calf as he ran aimlessly in circles. Adam leaped from his truck and dashed into the house, shouting Sally's name. After finding the house vacant, he bolted toward the holding pen and nearly tripped over the bottles and buckets, spilled milk, and formula still barely seeping from their openings. He immediately flew back into the house and contacted his foreman to reach all the available field hands. He called John at the Straight S, but there was no answer. Adam dashed into the pen and checked Al. "Hell!" Adam shouted as he heard the welcome sound of the brigade of trucks screeching to a halt in front of the house. Dust flew everywhere as he shouted desperate orders to the men while flying through the corral gate.

"Chris, take care of Al. He needs to be fed; keep trying to get a hold of John McKenna. Try his cell as well as the house." All the hands were assigned a section of pasture on the ranch to search. Adam announced the search was for Sally and Bill Tans, who was surely armed and dangerous. Each man was assigned a rifle or hand pistol. "I'm taking the east section which Tans is most familiar with." No one hesitated. A family member was missing.

"What are you going to do with me?" Sally asked nervously as Bill Tans yanked her from the truck and pulled her into an old cabin hidden in the hills located on the east side of the ranch. Sweat and tears rolled down her face, matting the loose hair on either side of her cheeks.

"No business of yours. It won't matter soon enough." He abruptly pushed her down on a chair and tied her swollen hands behind her to the wooden slats.

The rough rope cut into Sally's flesh. Blood trickled from the wounds. She closed her eyes, breathed in stale air, and tried calming down to think about an escape after Tans left the old cabin to retrieve some supplies from the truck. Adam's words haunted her thoughts. Tans was a killer, and he had nothing to lose by killing again. Her mind raced, and her eyes teared more profusely as she opened them, dust collecting on the dripping moisture. Her wrists throbbed from the pain. She couldn't comprehend why she was the target of this crazy man's aggressions.

Tans stumbled back into the cabin and slammed a duffel bag on the table. Sally jerked at the noise and coughed as the dust rose above the old wood and leather carrier. She stared at the desperate man, unable to speak. "Oh God," she whispered to herself, "please let Adam or my father find me."

"Let me take a good look at you, sweet thing," Tans sneered and flopped in a chair beside Sally. "I snagged a good one." He laughed hard, almost choking, and began to ramble as he grabbed a liquor bottle from the duffel bag. "You wanna know something funny? You almost stepped on me this morning when you got that horse of yours to go ridin'. I was down under all those weeds. I hid in them weeds all night," he angrily admitted but then calmed a bit. "I watched your little barrel race and you and Hamilton sleepn' together… would have gotten you sooner, but all my old buddies from the ranch showed up workin'…"

"That was why my horse was spooked. She should have trampled you to death." Sally struggled with the ropes with renewed energy, watching Tans guzzle the booze he'd brought. She mustered up the courage to question her captor. "Why do you want me anyway? What have I done to you?"

"Not you…but your daddy and Hamilton and Hollister and all the rest of those crooks trying to run these parts. They're stupid. Can't anyone see that? I know what's best for this land. I have worked in those lousy fields my whole life. By rights it should be mine. It was too easy for them!" Tans's anger escalated as he continued his tirade of drinking and babbling. "And then that old lady had to come back and move in with your daddy. She was going to spoil everything. I was sittin' pretty, your daddy payin' me off." He grabbed Sally by the arm. "And you! Why did you have to come back? Your mama was dead, finally. John was next. I waited and waited, and then *you* started asking all those questions. That old Wright woman scared easier than you." Tans dropped down in the chair, exhausted from the liquor and his half-baked explanations. "I could have had it all. Then Hamilton…" He laid his head on the table and passed out, the liquor bottle still secure in his grasp.

Sally writhed in pain as she tried to free herself from the ropes. Her blood dripped beneath the limp fingers as she finally abandoned her quest from sheer exhaustion. Tans eventually awoke. Without speaking, he jerked the ropes loose from Sally's bloodied wrists and poked a gun in her aching back.

The wooden door of the cabin splintered as Adam kicked in the barrier between himself and the contents inside, his rifle aimed and ready. But a quick study of the room revealed its vacancy. John dashed in after him and spotted the blood immediately. He instinctively bent down and squeezed the liquid between his callused fingers. Not waiting to hear the analysis, Adam bolted outside the cabin, searching for tracks.

"He's taken her somewhere else." Adam pointed out two sets of tracks heading toward the hills. "Come on, John. We've got to hurry before we lose the light."

Both Adam and John boasted excellent tracking records. They steadily climbed the hills with the force of a Texas hurricane. They were not certain about the lead Tans had on them, just the fact that the blood in the cabin was sticky and cool. They figured Sally would slow Tans down and, with luck and determination, they should catch up to them before the sun set.

"I can't understand it. We don't seem to be getting any closer. They are making good time!" John shouted as he and Adam trudged up the cactus-ridden hills.

"We'll find her, John. Maybe they had a bigger lead than we thought."

"No. Something's not right. We figured something wrong, and our advantage is the light. We lose that, and I'm afraid we lose." An hour later an abrupt rustling in the bushes alerted their already heightened senses, and Adam instinctively aimed his gun toward the sound.

Shots echoed ominously throughout the hills. Adam lowered his weapon only after he realized he had struck his target while Tans was trying to reload his rifle. An earlier shot whizzed by John, missing his head by inches. Both men darted toward an anguished cry but knew they were too late to retrieve any information when they glared upon Tans's open stare, blood pouring from his twisted head.

The two searched frantically before they realized Sally was not on the hill. "Where do we look now?" Adam yelled almost incoherently. "God, John, you don't think he wanted to die so we'd never find Sally…"

John grabbed him by the arm. "Calm down, son," he said, out of breath. "I want to find her more than life itself, but we have to keep clear heads." Adam nodded. "He didn't have time to hide her too far off the trail. Most likely, she's right around in this area. There were two sets of tracks up until it was impossible to discern between the rocks and footsteps. If he hid her, it has to be between here and where the rocks began." He stared at Adam. "Seem reasonable?"

"Yeah. I'll search below the ridge, and you take that rocky area."

"Let's do it."

Both men searched but found nothing. They regrouped beside the body of Tans. "I don't understand it. He didn't have that much time to stash her off the trail and keep ahead of us. Where can she be?" John slapped his hat against his leg and wiped his forehead.

"What about caves?" Adam suddenly thought out loud. "Tans used to work this area gathering stray cattle that wandered up in these hills, even when he worked for you, John. He had to know this terrain like the back of his hand. Our best bet is the ridge."

"Makes sense. No reception in these hills!" Adam yelled as he stuffed the useless cell back in his pocket. We need the help."

Again, the search proved fruitless. Night was descending, and, once it was dark, it would be impossible to find Sally until light. Adam and John shouted her name a thousand times but a haunting, hopeless silence was the only response they received. Even the night insects and animals would not retaliate and voice their opinions as to where Sally might be.

The reverberation of a hundred voices ascending the hills resembled music to John and Adam's ears. Workers from both ranches flooded the area as Adam spouted off quickly what had transpired and his theory of where Sally might be. The majority nodded and agreed as they spread out to resume the search. Lights flickered and darted like pinballs among the cacti and prickly bushes. A long, desperate hour passed before a voice among the crowd shouted, "Over here!"

Adam and John, along with other desperate ranch hands, raced to a grassy area beneath the ridge.

A hand pointed to the rocky ground. "Look here." The man bent down and pushed aside the weeds. "I almost missed it," he said. "There is another set of footprints going off in that direction."

Adam looked up at John and then spoke the obvious. "He had someone else with him the whole time. We were never chasing Tans and Sally. No wonder we couldn't catch up to them. He was purposely leading us away from the cabin."

"Yeah. She has to still be back there. We only saw two sets of footprints come out of that place."

Suddenly, loud voices and yelling echoed right below the ridge where the two men were perched. Both dodged toward the noise in time to see a half-beaten man held to the ground by the heel of a boot. "We found him hiding in one of these small caves. Had a hell of a time getting him out."

Adam lunged and grabbed him by the shirt, yanking him up from the ground. "Where is she?" he shouted, shaking him and then throwing him back down.

"I-I-I don't know," he stammered. "I don't." His eyes were desperate as he stared at the end of a gun pointed at his face. Adam grabbed him by the shirt with his other hand. "I swear!" the man screamed. "I met Tans at a bar the other night. He bought me a drink. Said he needed a favor. He showed me this cave and took me to a cabin. I didn't see what was in there. Oh God! Don't shoot me. I swear." He reached in his pocket and pulled out some crumpled bills. "This is what he paid me. Please, don't shoot me." Adam pushed the man away in disgust, the money trickling from his hands.

"Let's head back to the cabin, John. She has to be there. On the outside chance she's not, we'd better have the men stay here and search these caves. That lunatic Tans could have done anything."

A thorough but discouraging search of the cabin and its surroundings revealed nothing. Adam picked up one of the old wooden chairs and threw it across the room. "It's like she disappeared from the face of the earth!" he cried, frustrated.

"She's nowhere above ground, Adam. We just have to figure where Tans would have hidden her, someplace we'd never think to look."

"Wait a minute," Adam said out of breath. "Who built this cabin?"

"Tans did."

"Maybe a trap door…"

John and Adam frantically searched for a concealed door in the floor. They shoved around furniture, rugs, and overturned appliances. "Adam, the answer has to be close to this cabin. There's no other explanation."

The desperate men abandoned the cabin and discovered an old out-building built over some rocks in the bushes. John kicked in the door, and both of them tore the place apart, leaving nothing movable unturned. Again, they found only the rusty remains of an abandoned pump house. Adam kicked the dilapidated pump with his boot.

Both men looked back toward the house as they stepped out of the small enclosure and spotted the obvious at the same time. "I can't believe we were so stupid!" Adam shouted as he and John searched down the shaft of an old, dried-up well situated beside the cabin. Thorny vines had attached themselves to the rocks, breaking down parts of the oval wall that surrounded the ominous pit. John flashed a light toward the bottom of the hole to discover Sally lying sideways, her hands tied and her mouth gagged. A rope was attached around her waist, the end tied at the top of the well. Adam realized he could not just pull her up, as the rocks surrounding the pit were loose and they might fall on her in the process. He meticulously maneuvered himself down so as to not disturb the precarious rocks while John held the rope between his calloused hands. Adam finally reached Sally and gently removed the old cloth stuffed in her swollen mouth. Her body was covered in bruises and cuts. "I'd kill him again in a minute," he said under his breath as he untied the limp girl. He cradled her in his arms and held her against his chest. "She's alive!" His voice traveled up the shaft of the dungeon-like trap.

John hoisted Adam and Sally from the well, and both men rushed her to the hospital. She was in shock when they reached the emergency room, qualifying her status as critical. After hours of care, her condition succumbed to guarded. The sheriff questioned John and Adam about Tans and the unidentified man they'd dragged out of the cave on the ridge. The sheriff interviewed the doctor while John and Adam each privately searched their own conscious for an explanation.

"Are these the sins of the father—"

Adam interrupted, "It was not in our control. It never has been."

Sally finally opened her eyes after three days. Her thoughts jumped to Al. He too had faced death and survived.

John, Aunt Lucille, and Adam walked into the room, surprised to finally see Sally's eyes staring back at them. "My God, what happened?" Sally whispered, her eyes tearing. "Please tell me everything. Some things I can't remember… I need to know every detail."

Adam reached for her marred hand. He hesitated at the thought of bringing up an incident where guilt made the rounds and someone innocent was unfairly hurt.

"Please," Sally urged.

"Okay, but for now, just a quick version. Tans is dead. Your father, me, and most of the hands from both the ranches searched for you for hours before we finally found you in the well beside the cabin. He had carried you out to the well, lowered you down to the bottom with a rope, and then hired a man to go up into the hills with him. John and I thought we were chasing you until we discovered that you had never been with Tans. We doubled back and found you unconscious in that hole."

"Why me?" Sally asked desperately.

"I don't know, Sally. He hated me, and he hated your father. He must have scared Mrs. Wright into thinking that her husband was indeed murdered by John, or he out-and-out threatened her himself. He even hated your aunt. We may never know exactly what his motives were."

"Why did it matter to Tans that my aunt was back in Texas?"

"In his warped way, he probably figured there were more people in his way." Adam's eyes sought John for help.

"Honey, he thought he had Adam and me under his control, and then you came home and finally Lucille. He didn't have a hold on either one of you, and this was his way of…" Sally sighed heavily and rubbed her pulsating temples.

"Don't think about it now. You're safe, and so is Lucille."

Sally consented with a nod and lay quietly for a while, Adam's words swimming in her head. She still didn't understand why he had hired Tans in the first place. She was just so tired—"bone-tired" her mother used to say. It was hard to think.

"This is your third day in the hospital," Adam broke the silence. "You're going to be okay." He stroked her arm. "You were in shock when we brought you here. You have a broken wrist." Sally had noticed the cast and the pain immediately when she woke up.

"I'm glad to be alive." Adam handed her a tissue to catch a few of the streaming tears dripping from her chin. "Texas is giving me a rough time. I know how Al feels now. It ain't easy to stay alive here."

"You'll deal with this, Sally. There are professionals. They'll help you, and so will I. You will be taken care of. I could kill myself for leaving you..."

"No. It wasn't your fault. Tans told me he was there on my property the whole time. That's why Lady Grace was acting so agitated. He'd been lying in the fields all night waiting. So, you see, you couldn't have been with me every minute of the day. He would have eventually found me alone at some time. There is no one to blame, Adam, except Tans. Now that he's dead, I don't have anything to worry about, right?"

Adam walked out into the hall when they injected Sally with some medication for pain. He knew she deserved the whole truth. After Sally left the hospital he would answer all her questions, but for now he had a chance to make it up to her by providing her a safe house and by building some proper stalls for her horses.

Family and friends visited Sally often, allowing her to be kept up on all the latest about Al. She felt bonded with the small calf. After all, both of them had cheated death. Adam informed Sally that Chris was taking care of Al with Karen's help. He too possessed the instincts necessary to thwart Mother Nature. Dr. Lopez came by and said Al was okay! He even checked on Lady Grace and Lord Johnson, stating they grazed all day, their bellies bulging.

"Adam, did you ever look over the CDs?" Sally cautiously asked one day, sitting up in her hospital bed.

"Yeah. I would have waited, but even though regular session won't be opening until January, a special session was called. I needed some information. I also needed some answers."

"You still don't think my father—"

"I've discovered some interesting bits of history from those disks." Adam glanced at the clock on the wall. "I really have to go now." He kissed Sally on the forehead, barely brushing his lips against her skin, and breathed a heavy sigh. "You could have died. It makes a person think." Adam stared at her slightly sad eyes and pale face. "I want to see those eyes bright and vivacious again." He sighed. Sometimes independence and responsibilities are not conducive for good health.

"Adam, you are staring at me."

"I know," he said simply and left the room.

The rest of the morning passed slowly, and Sally's restlessness consumed her common sense. She ate with contemptuousness, refused to be entertained by television or hospital staff, and spoke aloud about the evils of boredom. Visitors remained her salvation.

Aunt Lucille moved nervously as she slowly entered the room and sat on a plaid hospital chair to the right of the bed. Adam positioned himself beside Sally, assuring John with his glances, and her father stood expressionless, grasping Lucille's hand.

"Are you up for a story?" Adam stroked her arm.

"Y'all are making me nervous. What's up?"

Adam began. "This is a story of how you and I fit into a place with a tumultuous history and scandalous past. When I began to buy up land to expand Hamilton Ranch, I discovered that original ownerships were somewhat questionable: titles unclear, unfinished paperwork, distorted boundaries, but I still pursued in an effort to enlarge Hamilton Ranch. After a while, I realized archaic laws and no informed government representation were my biggest hurdles. Therefore I fought for redistricting and better laws. After I was elected, John asked me, as a friend, if I'd help him out on a matter that he could not fully explain, which are the transfers you already know about. I helped John, and then Mr. Wright discovered some facts that should have been buried and forgotten years ago. He and Tans teamed up together. Wright soon died of a heart attack, and I have been paying Tans off for his silence ever since."

John looked up, surprised. "Adam, I had no idea. For five years he's been extorting you?"

"Well, let's just say his assistant foreman's job was a gift." Adam looked at Sally. "Those deliveries from the Straight S were also 'gifts' that were given to him to keep his mouth shut and to leave your father alone. He got it in his head a few months back that after

Wright had his heart attack John here had something to do with it. That crazy old fool thought you killed Wright to keep his mouth shut, John, and when Sally returned home, he began to demand ranch supplies in return for his silence. I had to make it look like the supplies were originating from the Straight S so he would think they were coming from you. Land, I suppose, was next on his agenda. He was greedy and insane."

"No wonder you didn't fire him. You were protecting my dad. So there was more to Tans's story," Sally said, disappointment in her tone.

"Yes." Adam looked at John. Hollister brought supplies and other goods to Tans's cabin where he was nesting. Hell, he could have been selling the goods on the black market." He looked at Sally. "That's how I knew where Tans took you."

"So, you see, your father really didn't know anything about supplies going out to the Hamilton Ranch. I bought all the goods myself and just had Hollister deliver it all. I guess that's when Karen met Chris." Adam turned to John. "I was just trying to protect you and keep a promise I'd made to a friend." He paused.

"This is the part where Hamilton Ranch becomes involved, because after the transfers were complete, John began allowing me to buy up some of the land that the corporation was supposedly getting ready to acquire. And then surprisingly, he began selling me parcels of the Straight S under the names we had just transferred. I couldn't pass it up."

Sally remained silent through all of Adam's explanation. She assessed her aunt Lucille as Adam unfolded his story. Her hands were white as she gripped the sides of the chair. Only after Adam finished did she finally relax. But he had left out the part about her father trying to take his ranch away. She wondered if this was the right time to bring it up, but, as though he were reading her mind, Adam flashed her a cautious look and she remained silent, not out of loyalty to him, she decided, but to her father. When her dad and aunt finally left, Adam remained.

"What was that all about? Now that they're gone, you can explain about why you think my dad may be trying to take away your land, even though he sold you parcels of the Straight S."

"In Austin, I constantly saw your dad's name all over land deals and legal papers right along with Captain King. There are sealed records from the past that no judge will touch with a ten-foot pole, even today. I thought these sealed records could jeopardize the ownership of my land. I was mistaken. This Captain King was the most unscrupulous man I have ever read about. He was not about to let anyone or anything get in his way if he wanted something. He was involved in murder, bribery, conspiracy—anything that would bring a profit. But he was a hell of a businessman and rancher. He was brilliant. We can attribute the founding of the Texas Longhorn to him and the discovery of Kleburg grass brought over from Africa. While he was sailing on one of his ships to Africa, he remained among the people and learned about their grasses and trees. Did you know that he instigated the use of Anthea trees as wind breaks in Texas? Yeah, brilliant, but undaunted in his ways to acquire anything he wanted. I can tell you that the railroads would not have been where they are now in Texas had it not been for Captain King. But land associated with King's name has always been under scrutiny by the Texas government. My land was acquired legally under the present laws of Texas by me every step of the way.

"Besides, what else do you want to know?

"I want to know why my father's name was on those land deeds and why Aunt Lucille was so nervous while you were telling your story. You obviously quit speaking at a very opportune time for her. Adam, while we were in Benning this last time she said there were things that my father had to tell me, things she couldn't."

"These were probably personal thoughts about their relationship."

"I think it's more. Was there something—"

Adam interrupted. "I don't know any more. I thought your father was trying to take away my land because his name was used simultaneously with Captain King's name and because of those sealed records. If you must know, I asked him about it, and he said as foreman of the Straight S he looked the other way many times to keep his job. He swore to me those sealed records were nothing but old legal matters and they could never affect Hamilton Ranch. He said he would never let that happen. His need and personal stake in the land is obviously greater than yours or mine. Is that what you wanted to hear, Sally? That your dad may not be as pure and innocent as you once thought? Knowing this makes you feel better?"

"You are always trying to turn around the fact that the truth is important to me." Sally rubbed her head. "We're partners, remember? Sealed with a kiss?" She managed a smile.

Adam sighed and sat in the chair beside her. "Sally, at the beginning of our relationship there were too many secrets between us. With Tans dead, the CDs safely hidden away never to hurt anyone, your father knowing the truth about Tans…the fact that we can lead normal lives now is enough for me. I do know some matters about the past but they have nothing to do with you or me or your father. I may use these facts in session when I need to but only to get my point across. I have used certain information to change a law but only for the better, for the benefit of everyone. The fact of the matter is there is always going to be someone out there knowing someone else's secret, but as far as it concerning you and me, it's over."

Sally looked at Adam. "It's not over."

Adam slammed his fist on the small table beside Sally's bed. She flinched and viewed Adam in a more cautious manner. "I meant what I said about taking everything that is dear to you away! Continue on this path, and it will lead to your own self-destruction. I will say it for the last time. There are secrets out there, but they have nothing to do with you. Leave it alone. You almost killed yourself already."

"I almost killed myself? Don't you think that is a little backward?"

"Start living for the future!" Adam turned from Sally. His anger emanated from their present situation, not anything she had done. If there was indeed something else to know, he would find out. "I need to go and speak to your father. I'll be back tomorrow."

"I can't give up seeking the truth."

"Well, I guess you have to do what you have to do."

Adam never returned to the hospital to visit Sally. He couldn't face her after another truth was unveiled by John at the hospital. He and Sally were indeed partners, and this secret was not his to tell. Until it was cleared up, he couldn't honor the terms of their contract and therefore could not face Sally. Her father and Aunt Lucille returned every day, singing Adam's praises, especially the day they arrived to bring Sally home from the hospital to the Straight S.

"Dad, I want to go back to my place today, not the ranch. It is my home now, and I just want to go home."

"You know you are always welcome—"

"I know, Dad, thanks."

When John and Sally pulled up to the once old, battered shack, Sally slumped in the truck and cried. The house's first floor was completely restored to its original elegance.

John stared at the building for a long time before speaking. "Must have taken a whole lot of men and a lot of overtime to do all of this in such a short amount of time." He whispered something else under his breath, his eyes closed.

"It was Adam, wasn't it?"

John sighed and wiped the moisture from his face. "I'm sure. The last time I saw him was when Dr. Lopez came over and declared Al fit and healthy and put him out to pasture with the other cows."

Sally was silently pleased and sad at the same time. Her job was over as far as Al was concerned. The dependent little calf didn't have to be bottle-fed any more. Sally smiled. "It's true what Adam said. Al is the sturdiest of the sturdy. Any other calf would still have had to ingest milk for a number of months to follow. Soon, y'all will be able to register him as a new breed of cattle. I'm so proud of you, Dad."

John reached for his daughter and held her tight.

"I'm glad Al is doing so well," she finally said.

"Thanks to you. Don't kid yourself, Sally. It was you that made the difference in that little fellow's life. I'm so very proud of you." John uncharacteristically smiled.

Sally noticed for the first time the tears on her father's face. "Dad, are you all right? What's wrong?" she asked, alarmed.

"Nothing, honey. I'm just glad you are out of the hospital and healthy again. Let's check out this house together. I'll get your bag."

Sally cautiously stepped into the refurbished house and instantly spotted a folded piece of paper lying alone on a small wooden table. She picked it up slowly and silently read the message. "Thanks for the help with Al. I hope this makes us even."

"It sounds so final," she said as she dropped the note. She'd felt a foreboding about Adam the day he left the hospital so angry, and she had a nagging suspicion that the talk he'd had with her father could be the reason she hadn't seen him again.

Sally insisted her father leave. She obviously had all the amenities: a bed, food, and a phone. Adam thought of everything…almost.

"Good-bye, honey. If you need anything, give me a call. Sure you won't change your mind about coming back to the Straight S with me?" John asked.

"I'm sure." Sally smiled. Even though she was beginning to more readily accept the relationship between her father and her aunt, she knew that this was her life now and she could never return to the home she once knew.

Sally cautiously walked into her room and plopped down on an old wooden bed with crisp, white sheets and an old fashioned quilt used as a spread partially turned down at one corner. She was already exhausted just from the short trip home from the hospital. She cried from loneliness and slept until the next morning.

As Sally yawned and sauntered into the kitchen she found an automatic coffee brewer. She smiled, thinking of how she made her dad buy one when she returned from New Orleans. Of course, there was a can of coffee sitting on the drain board and an electric can opener mounted under the cabinet. As Sally finished drinking her coffee, she again lay down from exhaustion, not waking up until late afternoon. Staring out the window of her bedroom, it was at that moment Sally realized how her father must have felt when he sat on the porch every morning before he began his laborious day. She wondered why he would try to deny her a feeling such as this. Sally noticed a new windmill by her stock pond already spinning and talking to the wind. She would have to capture this moment on canvas someday, as it would be embedded in her memory forever.

While Sally was checking the horses, Adam drove up to her refurbished abode. She returned to the house and opened the screen door as Adam was slamming the cabinets shut. "You haven't eaten anything?"

"I was just about to do that."

"You've been home since yesterday."

"And I've gotten the most wonderful rest...thank you."

"Sit and I'll make us both a sandwich. I could not believe it when John said you were out here alone. Karen, at least, should be staying with you."

"There's no point. I feel fine."

"I'm going to arrange for Karen to come out here with you."

"No. This is my home, but I don't want it if it comes with strings."

Adam silently continued preparing the food.

"You never came back to visit me in the hospital."

When Adam finished, he set the plates on the table. Sally mechanically sat in a chair across from him and began to eat. She stared at his every movement until he finally relinquished his silence. "I had things to do."

"That's not true."

"Sally," Adam began, "you want something I can't give you."

"The truth?"

"It's not my truth to tell anymore. You now have what you said you wanted. You have your land, your house. You wouldn't give this up for anything, would you, including me?"

Sally stood once again to face her partner. "Why should I ever have to make a choice? Why would it ever have to be you or the land?" She leaned against the counter. "By the same token, you wouldn't give up your ranch for me."

"Are you sure?" Adam put his plate on the counter, half of his sandwich in his hand. "I'm going to ask Karen to come out here and stay with you. You have a broken wrist for God's sake." He stopped in the doorway. "I also brought the pup today. He's in the truck. He'll make noise, anyway." Adam opened the screen door.

Exhausted, Sally spoke, intuition taking over. "My father said something to you in the hospital, Adam. He's told you something else you can't tell me. That's why you never came back. That's why you can't face me now."

Adam walked out, the door slamming behind him.

"There was a time when it was a possibility that you would have stayed here, you know," Sally murmured.

Adam fetched the pup and put it on Sally's porch. He placed the squirming dog gently down as though it took great care to transport something so small in comparison to him. "You want to make money from ranching? Is that really what you want? It won't be much, I can assure you, with this pittance of acreage, but so be it. I have about six Charlois calves born a few days ago; the mothers are refusing to feed, born too late in the season. You can have them for a fourth of fair market price. That will start you out." He searched the field for a quick analysis.

"Don't worry," Sally spoke up quickly. "I've already checked the cross fencing carefully. I am going to keep the stock on one side and grow some maize on the other along with some fruit trees. I'm having the field cut soon. I'm doing it for a third with Peterson, arranged it from the hospital. Two-thirds of my sale in the spring won't be a bad start."

"The cost of the grain can be put off till spring. Just go to the bank. They deal with farmers all the time. Use my name as a guarantor if you need to. The barn is ready—stalls on one side for the horses and mangers on the other for cattle. I had the old soil scooped to get rid of any parasites." Adam sighed. "You need a pickup—"

"Thanks…"

"Think hard, Sally. Poor decisions can cause failure." He turned abruptly and drove off down her dirt drive, yelling out the window, "Let my foreman know about the calves."

"The answer's yes!" Sally yelled, feeling surprisingly very low and very tired.

"A pickup?" she said to her squirming puppy. "I never thought about that. Dad gave me a small car, but on a ranch you really need a pickup. And, little mister, what about my job at the Straight S? I'll need money until I sell some cows in the spring, but if they have to be bottle-fed and there are six of them I won't have time to do both. I'll just have to train horses in the meantime. God, will there be enough hours in the day?" Sally couldn't afford regular calves at fair market price, and Adam knew that. His offer was a good one, but she would have to give up her job at the Straight S to have the extra time to care for the newborns. Now there would definitely be a struggle to find money to buy trees and plant orchards this fall. "Come on, little fella, let's go inside!"

Sally sat on her sofa, comprising a list of all the things she needed to do the next day. Even with the ranch on her mind, she still had to ponder over Aunt Lucille's words. What did they mean, and how could she find out without Adam getting wind of it? Adam obviously cared about her; he was always there, always helping, always worried.

Sally fell asleep on the couch and again woke to the sound of a vehicle pulling up in front of her porch. Voices and laughter traveled to Sally's tired ears, and she sighed.

"Sally!" There were many rapid, short knocks on the door as Karen's familiar, lively voice called her name. She was juggling suitcases while the pup was clawing and barking at the newly painted screen door. Adam patiently reached around the young girl and opened the door, grabbing the baggage from her fumbling hands. "Thanks." She smiled and immediately searched for her new roommate, discovering Sally on the couch.

She watched Adam take Karen's things into the second bedroom, his silence obviously deliberate. After his disappearance, Sally turned toward Karen and sighed. "I suppose Adam has talked you into staying here for a while."

"Isn't it great? I love it!" She paused and looked at Sally warily. "It's okay, isn't it? I mean you do have a bad arm and all."

"Of course it is," Adam answered as he walked back into the room. "Why don't you go put your clothes away, and I'll talk to Sally," he said.

"Adam, I told you I don't need anyone to stay with me," Sally said quietly, fearing Karen might hear.

"What did you eat for supper?"

Sally said nothing.

"That was easy." Adam walked out the front door, Sally intent on following him.

"I don't need to be looked after by a fourteen-year-old girl. I don't need to be looked after at all."

"Think about it, Sally, you were just released from the hospital, and you also have a broken wrist. You're not superwoman. There are chores to be done. Besides, she adores you…"

The pup was crying and clawing again at the screen door, apparently feeling abandoned at the moment. Sally let him out and picked him up lovingly. "As long as you know this isn't a permanent arrangement."

"We'll see." Adam began to walk off.

"No, we won't just see." Sally set the puppy down. "This is my land and my house. I have control."

"Didn't I invite you to buy calves from me? Didn't I fix up your place for you? Am I not providing you with help? Of course I am going to help. We are partners…sealed with a kiss."

"I want to make my own decisions out here without interference from you, even if I make mistakes." Sally's angry voice softened.

"You're here for God's sake. It's what you wanted."

Sally threw up her hands, wincing. "You're right and I know you care, but I also know you have your way too much in this partnership. Please tell me what my father told you in the hospital. I feel as though you are giving up our relationship out of loyalty to my father."

"You know that's not true."

"I don't know that."

"Then you're an even bigger fool than I thought." He walked to the truck and turned around. "It all means so much to you, doesn't it?"

"It's necessary to have that kind of attitude to survive, and you know it."

Adam reached in his pocket and walked back toward Sally with a piece of paper in his extended hand. "Here is a schedule of when you need to go to the hospital for your group therapy sessions. These meetings are important for your mental well-being. Don't miss any of them, Sally. They will help you heal."

Sally sighed, graciously receiving the paper and turned toward the house, not bothering to respond. Adam reached for her arm. "You are forgetting a lot of what I told you that last day I saw you in the hospital."

"I have not forgotten that the last day you saw me was not my last day in the hospital."

Adam released her arm and left.

Sally peered down at the pup chewing on her sock. "Ow!" she screamed, as a sharp tooth gnawed its way through the thin material. Sally scooped him up with just one hand and walked into the living room.

"Are you and Adam mad at each other?" Karen asked.

"Not angry as much as trying to understand each other." Sally sighed. "What would you like for supper?"

The two girls were sitting at the kitchen table just finishing up some fried chicken when Sally began the conversation. "Remember when you first told me about some supplies the Straight S used to deliver to Hamilton Ranch?"

"Sure. That's the night I told you about Chris." Karen smiled.

"Yeah, that was the time." Sally picked up the two empty plates with one hand and set them in the sink. She quickly answered the anticipated question. "I used to wait tables in New Orleans."

"Cool!"

Sally shook her head and continued. "Anyway, I remember thinking back then that you were pretty perceptive for your age, and now I'm wondering if you could possibly be of some help to me in the future?"

Karen's eyes lit up at the prospect. "Yes! I'll do anything!"

Sally stared at her keenly. "This will have to be between you and me only. Karen, you can't even tell Chris, because then it may get back to Adam and I don't want him to know what I'm doing, okay?"

"Sure."

"I mean it, Karen. You can't tell anyone what we'll be doing."

"Is this part of the understanding each other thing?"

Sally sighed. "Yes, I suppose he is, but I can't worry about that now."

"But what happened between you two? I thought y'all had already passed the understanding and were into the love stage." Karen said dreamily.

"So did I, but I guess the past relives itself. I was about your age when Adam walked away from me the first time."

"Tell me about it, please," the young girl pleaded.

"Let's go in the living room," Sally suggested. As the two were seated comfortably on the couch, Sally related all the stories and memories of her childhood with Adam. "Adam was my rock. When I was a young girl entering junior high, I was awkward to say the least. I lacked the confidence to be popular. I felt as though I didn't have the right. I wasn't close to my mother, and of course the Straight S kept my father extremely busy. I was alone a lot during my childhood.

"Adam was a friend of my father's, and we met one day on the ranch and kind of connected. He walked up to me while I was sitting on a fencepost and introduced himself. He asked me the kind of questions young girls love to be asked. Who was my favorite actor? What did I do in my spare time? Would I like to join a 4H club he sponsored. He could take me to the meetings and help with the animals I would raise. He was the brother I never had, the defender of my youth. He and my father were very close, and I suppose Adam must have felt an obligation of some sort, so he took me under his wing and suddenly I didn't feel as lonely or as awkward. I felt as though I belonged."

"Were you in love with him?" asked Karen.

"Are you kidding? I didn't know what love was. I was way too young. I just wanted to be an ordinary kid who did ordinary things. Adam made that possible. He used to take Lisa, my good friend, and I to the movies, the café in Benning, the mall in the big city. And if he said he would pick us up at a certain time, he would. He was never late, not once."

"How long were you and Adam friends?"

"That's a tough one. Adam considered us good friends until I left for college, but when I entered high school I noticed that my feelings for him were changing. He was usually my confidant, but how could I approach him about how I felt? For a couple of years I struggled with the confusion, but then I started to feel awkward again, and I became very angry. I took out my anger on Adam, but he always smiled, never complained and was still there for me. I look back on it now and clearly I was falling for him, but that was not his role in my life, and I was just a silly high school girl with silly high school feelings."

"It took a long time before y'all got together."

"Well, sometimes it seems as though that is where our life is heading, and then the next minute, I wonder about my feelings and his and if they are truly real." Sally faced Karen. "We agreed to be partners anyway. That is a good start."

"I love this story. Tell me more."

"Well, once when I was in eighth grade Adam bought a new horse. He rode it over to the ranch and asked me if I wanted to take a ride. Well, of course I did. The horse was seventeen hands high, a good height for a thoroughbred. The only problem was the horse was a stallion to be used for breeding purposes. As good as I was on a horse, handling a stallion was for the expert rider, as the blood runs hot through an animal not yet gelded. Finding such a horse difficult to control at times, Adam reached down and swooped me up on the back of the horse with one lift. Holding on around his waist, Adam maintained control of the animal as we cantered through the fields. Surprisingly we rode to the 4-H barn, where many of my friends from high school cared for their animals. Adam entered and then cantered to the end of the barn, where he stopped in front of Mary Louise, my sworn high school enemy. She was the only one in the barn. Then he did the strangest thing. Adam asked me to dismount and reached for Mary Louise to give her a ride. Mary Louise didn't know what to do. The terror in her eyes made me laugh, but Adam reached over and lifted her on the back of the horse and the last thing I heard was, 'Hold on tight. This is going to be a ride you'll never forget.' Adam galloped into the field, Mary Louise screaming. I couldn't help but laugh my head off. When they returned, Mary Louise gratefully slid off the horse and retreated to her stall. I again remounted and Adam brought me home. As he was about to leave, I had to ask him what really just happened. He said there was a rumor going around the barn that Mary Louise was the best rider and that certain members couldn't ride their way out of a paper sack. He said he couldn't wait to hear the next rumor that surfaced and was positive this one would be laid to rest."

"That was great! Do you have more?"

"No more stories tonight. Let's get some ice-cream."

Sally thought about how nice it was to have someone to talk to in the evening. Perhaps there was wisdom in this arrangement after all. As eleven o'clock approached, Karen began to show signs of fatigue, so Sally told her to go to bed and assured her they'd talk tomorrow. Both had to get up extra early the next day to load up the Charlois calves from Hamilton Ranch.

Chapter Eight

Youth finds special bonds where others might not look:
In a room, or in a book, or in that special tree,
A place where no one understands,
A place where young may flee.

I find my spot on farm's crisp edge.
Beneath the windmill's grasp
I lie and dream and even sleep.
Their shadows form my mask.

The shadows move as day goes by.
I move to beat the heat.
I sit upon the edge of ponds
And slowly soak my feet.

I'll leave today when life will call
To happiness or sorrow.
I'll study, work, and learn to live.
I reserve my place for tomorrow.

Sally woke up feeling better than she had for a long time. After drinking some coffee, making breakfast, and staving off Karen's questions about when she was going to need her "keen perceptiveness," Sally felt ready for a full day. Her arm bothered her a bit, but she had not been careful about elevating it as the doctor had instructed when he sent her home. The antibiotics were somewhere between the hospital and her new bedroom; the cost to replace them was an issue at this point. The two drove Sally's small car over to the Straight S and exchanged it for a pickup and trailer. They arrived at Hamilton Ranch around 6:00 a.m. and knocked on the door of the foreman's office. He directed them to the east barn on the Sierra Section of the ranch.

Sally laughed at the calves as they wobbled about in the small holding pen. She and Karen leaned on the corral post, watching them intently. One of the hands opened the gate, and Sally examined each calf carefully and expertly. They were all in fine condition and were loaded up with ease onto the trailer. A ranch's reputation was always at risk with the sale of livestock, so Sally knew she was getting good calves.

"That'll do it," the hand said as he pushed the steel pin through the lock on the trailer. "These are fine calves—almost as good as that one everybody's making all the commotion over. Seems it's all anyone ever talks about these days."

Sally's heart tugged at her common sense. "Do you know where that new calf—"

The hand instantly smiled. "You too, huh? He's near the main house in a small pasture with the other calves. I wish I had all the attention that little critter was getting. Come to think of it, I think some reporters are out there now asking questions and taking pictures for that Texas magazine. He is a good-looking piece of livestock. A possible new registered breed—it's kind of hard to believe. Why don't you go over and take a look?" The hand tipped his hat and mounted his horse.

Sally desperately wanted to see Al. She missed him terribly, so, at Karen's urging, they drove to the pasture and walked up to the enclosure, leaving the calves in the trailer. Reporters dotted the fence. A few brave ones stood in the field taking pictures while Adam held the calf with a lead rope connected to his halter. Sally noticed that in her absence Al had been branded. The men and women from the magazine shot out questions and wrote furiously in their notebooks while she and Karen stared at the sight until Adam finally seemed to have had enough and gently dismissed them. The demeanor of Al was incredible. A normal calf would have acted up and refused to graze under these circumstances. Al, with all he had been through, had shown incredible tolerance to the extraordinary incidents surrounding him. Adam noticed Sally and easily led Al over to the fence for her to inspect.

"He's doing so well." Sally smiled. The little calf's eyes widened as he instantly recognized her voice and nuzzled up to her. She squatted down and petted him for a long while before Adam spoke.

"He remembers you."

The reporters all dispersed, and Sally watched their vehicles drive away. The calf was licking her face, and she laughed as she nuzzled up to Al's neck.

"I think this is the picture they should have taken for their magazine," Adam said, staring at Sally and Al.

"Yes, well, we'd better be going," Sally said, standing up, tears in her eyes.

Al began bawling as Sally turned away. He followed her up the fence line and his eyes begged her not to go. She walked away.

"I have to unload these new calves and get the trailer back to the Straight S."

"Let me get some of the boys to come over—"

"No. Thank you," Sally said, emphatically gaining her composure.

Adam noticed Sally was favoring her arm and hopped the fence. "Your fingers are swollen twice their size."

"We've been busy today. I'll elevate it when I get home."

"I'm going to send someone with you to unload the calves and return the trailer."

"I don't need help. I'm managing just fine."

Karen spoke up. "We could ask Chris to come over and give us a hand." She raised her eyebrows inquisitively at Adam.

"You see, your partner here feels she has the right man for the job."

"You're a traitor!" Sally whispered to Karen before Adam took her by the hand to get his phone from the truck.

Karen returned to the Straight S truck, waiting for Chris to arrive, leaving Sally alone with Adam. "You've taken on many additional duties at your place. Let Karen help you—that's what she's there for."

"Adam, can I see those disks we found at Mrs. Wright's office?"

"I already told you those disks are risky for a lot of people living around here. Why would you want to see them now?"

"I just do."

"Well, you can't, Sally. They're in a safe place where no one will be hurt by them."

"Okay. Fine." Sally turned to leave.

"Isn't your land enough to keep you busy? Doesn't that satisfy you?"

"Yes, I suppose it does." Sally turned back and smiled. "The land really is a Godsend. Thanks for the low price on the calves."

Work on the small ranch was hard but wonderfully rewarding. Sally missed Adam, but she was so busy every day that at night sleep came easily as exhaustion dominated her will to continue working.

Money was a problem already though. She had three horses to train from one of the riding clubs in Benning, but that money wouldn't filter in for a few months and she was low on grain for the horses now as well as the calves. Six months of land payments lay in the bank, which she would not even consider touching. The bank advanced her a small loan to purchase the grain, but she had to go in halves instead of thirds with a nearby farmer because she didn't have the tractor to plow the maize once it was planted. Even going in halves meant that she would have to borrow his tractor and plow the rows between the crops a few times a week. Ultimately, it meant less money and less grain at harvest. Maybe riding lessons was the answer; she knew of several young people who enjoyed the horse shows in Benning every month. The Abilene rodeo was also coming up and some of the young girls in the area already entered the junior horse riding competition. Many would want some last-minute pointers on what to do in the rink and how to show well, and that would mean immediate cash.

Karen brought up an interesting fact when the two were eating dinner one evening,. "You know I can't believe it is the middle of August. What a summer! It's been great, and the rodeo is coming up soon. It will be the perfect end to the perfect summer." Karen paused. "I'm sorry. That was thoughtless. I guess you can't ride in the rodeo after all this year."

"Oh, I don't know. We'll see. I still have a while."

"I talked to Dad yesterday and he said I have to go back to the Straight S to live at least two days before the new school year begins which is in two weeks. I don't want to leave. I usually have such a boring summer, but you've let Chris come over and we've trained horses and plowed fields. I've written all of this down in my diary, you know—the greatest summer of my life."

Sally looked at Karen, half listening to what she said until the last sentence. "What did you say?"

"I said I've written all of this down in my diary."

"You're a genius."

"What did I say?"

"You know, my mother used to keep a diary. If there were any secrets in her life, it would be in that book. I wonder what she did with it. I know my father put all of her things in one place..." Sally was silent for only a moment before exploding with renewed energy. "Karen, I'm now going to need those perceptive instincts you have before I have to relinquish you to the new school year."

"Is this what you were talking when I first came to live here?"

"It sure is." Sally smiled triumphantly. "First of all, Adam is leaving for a two-week special session in Austin early tomorrow. I heard it from one of the hands when we loaded the calves a few days ago. We need to get near the Hamilton Ranch—that's my job—and we need to get near the Straight S—that's your job."

"That's a little backwards, right?"

"No. Listen. We've only got two weeks because you'll be gone soon and Adam will return. They know me out at Hamilton Ranch because of Al and of course they did all the work on this house and all. They wouldn't suspect me poking around. They know you at my dad's place because your dad is a foreman and would not suspect you poking around there, whereas, the other way each of us would be under scrutiny at this point in our lives. Understand?"

"I guess so, but even if I don't this sounds really great."

"Good. Tomorrow after we feed the calves, and before the Winston girl comes for her first riding lesson, you go over to the

Straight S and tell my Aunt Lucille that you need to look up in the attic for some furniture I need for my house. Let me see…what is in that attic?" Sally thought a minute and smiled. "Tell her I said something about an old desk that I want as I am planning on buying a computer and I need a piece of furniture to set it on. While you are up there, you'll see in one of the corners of the attic a large trunk. It has all of my mother's old belongings in it. Open it up and look for a diary. I don't know if it's going to be like a traditional one, but it should have daily entries. Karen, you can't let Lucille know you are doing this. I know my aunt. She won't climb those stairs. If she asks what is taking you so long just tell her that you're removing, carefully, all the junk out of the desk before you bring it down, okay?"

"This sounds like so much fun!"

Sally sighed. "Karen, this is serious business."

"I know, but you have to admit, it is exciting. What are you going to do at the Hamilton Ranch?"

"I'm going to get my hands on those disks. At one time, Adam was very willing to let me see them. I just have to believe he still feels the same way, or I would be considered a thief."

"I never thought of it that way."

"You know, if I get caught, I don't think Adam will understand why I'm doing this."

"He'll understand, and besides, how can we possibly get caught when we're so good?"

Sally smiled. "Who's got 10:00 p.m. feeding duty for the calves?"

"I do. Then you've got the 2:00 a.m."

"I was afraid of that."

The next morning regular duties were performed and each girl set out on her own mission. Sally arrived at Hamilton Ranch, knowing Adam would not be there. She told one of the hands that Adam had left something for her on his desk and that he had said to go ahead and get it. Sally carefully entered Adam's office and inspected her surroundings. She knew he had a safe in there but did not know where. When he had retrieved the disks before for her, Sally was not in the room, and he had never mentioned their whereabouts.

She noticed his office was very dark; it had massive furniture and tin ceilings. The ambiance was foreboding, but her motives drove her without thought of consequence. Sally searched behind pictures and for false bottoms in desk drawers. It seemed she had looked everywhere when she glanced down and saw a slight elevation in the forest green area rug under his desk. She reached down and lifted the edge. There, almost completely camouflaged with the wooden floor, was a small safe, the dial receding into the door so as not to bulge under the carpet. *Clever,* she thought, but now that she had found it, how was she going to get the combination? Sally knew Adam would not leave the combination to the safe just lying around, as her eyes canvassed the room. Realizing she had been in his office a tad too long to just get some papers off his desk, she quickly covered the floor safe with the rug and walked nonchalantly out of the house, pretending to read some documents she had brought in her pocket. She smiled at the hand, who was sitting in his truck, one foot dangling from the doorway.

"Sorry I took so long. I began to read the instructions Adam had left when it dawned on me that you may be waiting for me to leave." She smiled. "I'll return these in a few days. See ya!" *Brilliant,* she thought to herself. *Now I'm expected to return.*

Sally met Karen at the house, anxious to hear what the young girl had to say.

"The trunk was filled with old clothes, pictures, and papers," Karen said, with pent-up excitement. "I did what you told me to do and began to look through them, but then your aunt yelled up to me that she had gotten a hand to help me carry the desk down. So I had to quit looking. She kind of wondered why I had ridden a horse to pick up a desk, so one of the workers brought it over in the back of a pickup."

"I didn't think of that. We'll have to be more careful in the future."

"There was still so much more to go through, but I was forced to leave when Lucille sent someone to help me—he helped me right out of the investigating business."

"It sounds like your excursion was the same as mine. We both ran out of time. We've got to figure out a way to get you back up into that attic without drawing suspicion." Sally rubbed her sore arm.

She was sweating and tired. "Come on, let's saddle up Lady Grace. My student will be here in about fifteen minutes, and I'll teach you how to give lessons."

The two girls were brushing down the horse and chatting about their morning adventure when the nine-year-old arrived. The lesson went well, and Sally was paid for the hour's work.

"Well, Karen, money don't come easy!" She waved the bills around in the air with satisfaction. It wasn't much, but it would buy several bags of grain. Sally had two other lessons that day, and hopefully the kids would spread the word and continue to come. Sally again favored her arm to the point of alerting Karen.

"I'll finish up here. Go on ahead."

Sally smiled at her thoughtfulness. "I'll go in, but it will be to make us lunch." She put her hand on Karen's shoulder. "I can still pull my weight around here."

The day was long and hard, but again rewarding. The other two children showed up for their lessons, which meant Lady Grace had to be saddled again and brushed and given extra oats for her trouble. Lord Johnson had missed the mare during the last lesson and ran the length of the fence, impatient for her return.

Sally mentally went over her schedule—three lessons a day for an hour each, training each horse at least four hours a day, and plowing the fields with the weather as dry as it was in the evening so as not to expose the maize and freshly dug soil to the hot sun. Sally sighed. Then she had to feed the calves every four hours, but Karen was a lifesaver and the thought of losing her in a couple of weeks weighed on her mind, as did Adam.

Both girls were gratefully sitting on the front porch one evening while Karen was playing with the puppy, his growling noises muffled by the old sock he had in his mouth. The sun was setting, the insects were singing, the horses were grazing, and all the animals were taken care of, at least for a while.

Exhausted as she was, Sally was still trying to figure out a way to return to the Straight S and the Hamilton Ranch and how to get the combination to Adam's safe. "You can tell Aunt Lucille there is more furniture up there in the attic that I need, okay?" She finally blurted out loud.

"Sure," Karen said, unconcerned, still playing with the pup.

Sally began to feel a bit guilty about Karen's involvement. "Is all of this all right with you? I mean, I don't want you to do something you don't feel is right. I won't be the least bit hurt if you don't want to do this."

"What are you talking about? I've never done anything so exciting in all of my life! Of course all of this is all right. I just hope I don't mess up!" Karen looked at Sally eagerly, letting the little Heeler get the better of her sock.

"Don't worry. You'll do fine." Sally sighed.

After a few moments of silence Karen shooed the pup off the porch and sat next to Sally. "What exactly is it we're looking for? I know a diary, but what's in it?"

"Honestly, I don't know."

"But it's important?"

"Yeah, it's really important to me."

"Are you going over to the Hamilton Ranch tomorrow?"

"Well, there's no use going unless I have a pretty good idea of where the combination to that safe is. That's all I've been thinking about for days."

"What if Adam doesn't have it written down?"

"He has it written down all right. What if he died or something? His legal matters…" Sally suddenly stopped talking and smiled.

"What?"

She sat up straight. "His legal matters are all on disks. He said that when we were in the real estate office looking for Wright's records. Adam said, 'Mine should be in such order.'" Sally smiled at Karen. "I know where Adam's legal disks are! I saw him using them one day when I was over there. I'll just bring them back to the Straight S and use my old computer in the foreman's office and get the combination to the safe off them. I'll return them before Adam returns home. Simple." Sally looked at Karen. "All is still going strong. I can drop you off at the ranch and then bring you home from the Straight S after I've looked at the disks. I've just got to figure out a way to get to Adam's house a third and final time. I'll cross that bridge when I come to it. We'd better get busy around here. I'll do the dishes and you feed the pup."

The next day Sally drove to the Hamilton Ranch on the pretense of returning the papers to Adam's desk. The same hand waited for her to leave, unaware she was packing a plastic case full of hard drive disks under her cotton jacket. She had phoned her father to ask if she could use the computer to set up some software before her own arrived at the house in a week or two.

Using her own ranch work as an excuse to leave, Sally visited only briefly with her dad and aunt. She quickly told them about the Charlois calves, and they expressed a sincere desire to come over and see them sometime. Karen and Sally glanced at each other as they jumped into the truck.

The information Sally needed was indeed on one of the disks found in Adam's house, but, feeling a tad nervous with someone else's property, she decided to drop by the Hamilton Ranch and get rid of the hot merchandise. It would be even harder now to think up an excuse to visit Adam's house for the fourth time and Sally kept telling herself all of this was necessary because no one would tell her the truth. Karen accompanied Sally as they drove up to the Hamilton main house. Of course, it was locked, so the young girl sat on the steps as Sally tracked down one of the hands. He unlocked the residence, still as patient and polite as the first time Sally visited.

"I'm really sorry." Sally lied. "But one of my own inventory sheets must have gotten mixed up with those papers I returned."

"It's all right, ma'am. No problem."

On the way over to the Hamilton Ranch, Karen told Sally she'd searched for the book but to no avail. They smiled at each other as the small back seat of Sally's car sported an end table and antique sewing cabinet.

"Well," Karen said, "I had to bring something back!"

Again, the day on the ranch was long but rewarding. The lessons went well, as did the training of the horses and the feeding of the calves. There never seemed to be a spare second. Money was still short and Sally's arm ached constantly, but ranch work continued without a break and the young girl loved every exhausting minute of it. This was her destiny.

Sally continued to attend her therapy sessions at the hospital and had to admit they were a tremendous aid in her peace of mind concerning the situation with Tans even though it was an hour drive over and back and she could hardly afford the time. At first, she was having nightmares, but now the incident was fading into her past with ease as she learned how to deal with the situation by talking to others who had experienced the same kind of ordeal. While Sally was leaving a session one evening, she bumped into the doctor who cared for her in the hospital. "Sally, how are you doing?"

"Fine. Great. Couldn't be better." She tried to leave quickly.

"Let me just take a quick look at your arm while you are here."

"No, I'm fine, really. I'm in kind of a hurry."

The doctor ignored her excuse and lifted the arm supporting the cast. "This doesn't look so good," he said, concerned. "Come by my office first thing in the morning and let me take a better look."

Sally sighed. "Sure. I'll be there." She knew deep down inside there was something wrong with her arm but hadn't wanted to admit she'd have to take the time to do something about it. *Well, an hour or so,* she thought, *what would it hurt?*

Sally couldn't believe her bad luck. She checked into the hospital for intravenous antibiotics because there was an internal infection in the break of her arm. She felt at this point she had no control over a very serious situation. She couldn't help but think of the irony of her mind healing and her body not obediently following. Sally was forced to call her father so he could arrange everything for her, including someone to stay with Karen. Aunt Lucille drove to the hospital immediately, and John joined her later. They stayed until visiting hours were over and spoke mostly of Aunt Lucille's adjusting to ranch life. She said it brought back all the sweet memories of her youth and she was basking in the sunlight and quietness of her surroundings. Sally recognized her poetic way of expressing herself from the letters she thought her mother had written to her. Whatever the reason, they were a work of art, and she was grateful when Aunt Lucille had agreed to keep the correspondence until Sally felt the need to possess them once again. She was truly happy that her aunt was acclimating herself so quickly to the ranch after all those years in New Orleans.

It was quite late, but Sally remained restless. Her thoughts were with her livestock and Karen and everything that accompanied the responsibility of her small ranch. It seemed as though her lifeline was cut and she was just barely surviving away from her land. Suddenly, someone knocked on her door and entered the room.

"Adam is that you?" Sally asked, surprised. "You look awful. Aren't you sleeping at all in Austin?"

"We've had several late-night sessions. I drove down here after the last one let out. I have to be back in Austin at 9:00 a.m."

Sally glanced at the illuminated clock on the wall. It was 1:00 am. "You can't drive back tonight."

"I have to. Your father called and told me you were in the hospital again. I had to see you."

"He shouldn't have bothered you. I'll probably be out tomorrow. It really is good to see you, though."

Adam pulled up a chair and sat beside Sally's bed. "I thought Karen was going to help you feed those calves."

"She is helping me. You were right. I couldn't do it without her."

"So what happened to your arm? Your father said you were doing too much…"

"No. I did more every day when I worked at the Straight S."

"Sally, I'm really tired, and the session is not going well. Don't beat around the bush. What else are you doing out there on your place?"

"Adam, what I have to do to make a go of it. I have a small cash flow problem, so I'm training some horses, giving a few riding lessons, some plowing…"

"Besides feeding those calves every four hours? Sally—"

"I needed the cash."

"You mean you don't have enough to—"

"It's not your business, Adam. My finances are personal."

"Sally, I care for you. Whatever obstacles you have we can work them out together."

I'll be out by tomorrow, and I'll manage. I didn't take some antibiotics, that's all. I admit it, okay, yes it was stupid, but I work hard at my place and I love it. I wouldn't have this idiotic broken wrist if it wasn't for—"

"Your curiosity."

"My interest in the truth."

"Name it whatever you want. You can't even handle fifty acres with help—"

Sam, please understand. I can do this. I can!"

"Keep your voice down. Listen, I'm going to lend you some money—"

"I won't take it. I don't want your help. I know what my limitations are now."

"That's a laugh. You know what your limitations are? Look around you. Think about it. You have been in the hospital three times since you've been home. It is exactly because you don't know what your limitations are that you are in here. You should just relinquish this notion that you must control everything in your life."

"That's not fair. There have been extenuating circumstances, and you know it. I could be dead, you know. Think of how I've survived."

Adam reluctantly peered at his watch. "I have to get going soon."

"I know we are arguing, but I don't want you to go."

"I won't be back, you know."

"I won't keep you. It's so late. My partner has to get some sleep."

"I have to return to Austin. I know you are not going to understand why you have to do this, but I don't have time to explain. Have the owners pick up those horses and tell them if they still need to be trained that we'll do it at Hamilton Ranch for the agreed price. I won't compromise your word. Cancel the lessons. Have Karen help you with the calves, and you call whoever is going in halves with you on your winter wheat to come out to your place and plow those rows himself, even if you have to reduce your portion to a third. Concentrate on those calves, but do get Karen to help. You may have to relinquish your land—"

"How can that be?"

"It is a small price to pay to save your life."

"It would destroy my life."

"That may be what you think now. I'll have one of the hands bring Al over to your place and I'll pay you to care for him. In fact, I will give you an advance for keeping Al. I wouldn't want him to starve to death. He loves being out in the pasture and you have great grasses on your land. I'll be back in a week." He left abruptly.

Sally enjoyed teaching her lessons and training the horses and wondered why Adam wanted these changes. Why shouldn't she pay her dues like the rest of the ranchers?

Sally spent a day and a half in the hospital. John picked her up, and Sally requested he stay a while when they pulled up to the house. Al was in the holding pen already, and she made an immediate note to put him out to pasture. She was ecstatic at his return.

After the coffee brewed, both she and her father sat on the porch to drink. Karen was feeding the calves in the barn and had waved enthusiastically when the truck drove past her and up the dirt road to the house.

"Be sure to take those pills this time."

"Don't worry. I am never going to be in a hospital again. I've learned the hard way about that one. Dad, I do need to ask you a question. You don't know how much I need an answer for my peace of mind." She held one of his large hands in hers. "Did you tell Adam something about me when I was in the hospital?" She looked intently at her father, waiting for a response.

He sighed. "I've kept some things from you in the past, Sally. I know it's hurt you, and I never meant for that to happen. The truth of the matter is, it did, and there's nothing I can do to take that away but it's in the past. As for now, Adam and I had a serious discussion in the hospital. I told him some things I've never told anyone in my life, things I'm not particularly proud of."

"But what has that got to do with me? Adam said that he would not hold anything against me that concerned you. I asked him."

"It's not that, honey. You see, you and I are exactly alike and, God help us, you are heading in the same direction that I took so many years ago. He's just trying to protect you, knowing how the decisions I made in the past almost destroyed me."

"What are you talking about, Daddy? You're scaring me."

John reached over and hugged his daughter. "Don't be afraid." John held her tightly for a few minutes before continuing. "I'm sure he feels like he's doing the right thing…"

"What right thing? It's my life, and I don't understand why Adam won't just be honest with me."

"I'm sure he's just trying to protect you."

"From what?" Sally yelled.

"I guess from yourself," John said quietly. "Like someone should have done for me twenty-two years ago."

Sally had no response. She knew the ultimate answer to her question lay waiting in those disks at Adam's house and in her mother's diary. She tenderly placed her arm around her daddy protectively. "It's all right." They sat on the porch and each drank another cup of coffee as both peered toward the edge of her property, their view stretching toward the windmills beyond her own.

Karen returned from the barn, and John left in his pickup, taking back to the Straight S the woman who had stayed with Karen while Sally was in the hospital. Sally hugged Karen and told her that tomorrow was the day they would find out something or she would for sure go crazy if, in fact, she had not already done so. She explained to the young girl about the horses and the lessons, much to Karen's disappointment, as she had taken over the job in Sally's absence. They consoled each other by saying that maybe when Sally's arm was fully healed they could begin the activities once again. Karen also made a small comment about the bossiness of Adam and that she hoped it wouldn't rub off on Chris.

Sally nervously drove to the Hamilton Ranch the next day in her small car. This time she could say that some special instructions for Al were in Adam's office. With all the attention that calf was getting, Sally knew that it was a very plausible story. She found the hand out at the barn wrestling with some calves; he was trying to load them in the shoots to be branded. Several of the other men were laughing and teasing the poor fellow, but then at last they decided to give him a helping hand. Sally knew she couldn't disturb him in the middle of his work, so she just relayed the message to one of the hands standing by a gate that she would return that afternoon after lunch to retrieve the instructions about Al. He agreed as best he could, cursing about a bull getting loose in the pasture during the fall and that summer branding was the worst of all.

Sally returned home, fed the calves, and played with Al. He was growing by leaps and bounds, his remarkable disposition accompanying his progress. She was so grateful to have Al, and her arm felt so much better after leaving the hospital.

Sally glanced at her watch to see if it was time to return to the Hamilton Ranch. Karen asked if she could go along, and even though it was against her better judgment, she agreed. The two of them departed for their destination in early afternoon. The hand was waiting for them on the porch and opened the door politely, but the two entered the dark area with consternation.

"I don't know why, but I'm a little nervous," Karen confessed.

"I'm a little nervous, too. This is my fourth time here, and I'm afraid I'm pushing my luck."

"I'm afraid both of you ladies are pushing your luck, and it just ran out." Adam closed the door behind them. "I could ask what you are doing here, but unfortunately I have already guessed." He walked to his chair and cautiously sat down, never breaking the stare between Sally and himself. Adam picked up the phone and called for Chris to come to the main house. He addressed Sally. "I understand your passion to use whatever means possible to seek answers you feel are essential to your existence, but to encourage a young girl to be dishonest? That is unforgivable."

Karen spoke up, trying to defend her friend. "But Mr. Hamilton—"

Adam slammed his hand on the desk, breaking the hold his eyes had on Sally. "You don't understand the implications of your actions right now."

Chris arrived and escorted Karen back home. When Adam heard the truck take off, he looked up, moving only his eyes, his gaze searing Sally's inner being. "Didn't you think that the people who work for me would call and tell me everything that was going on around here while I was away? And didn't you think that I would question the fact that you were picking up imaginary papers from my desk—not once, but three times—and that you, of all people, needed instructions on how to care for Al?"

"You arrived here some time ago?"

"Yes."

"Then you are as dishonest as I am. We are the same."

"I talked to your father and Lucille. It seems that Karen has been going over to John's place and searching the attic. I can't believe you involved that young girl in all of this. I can't believe you would try something like this against me."

"It didn't have to be against you. It didn't have to be that way. You set those ground rules. You have been fighting me since I came back home, and I still don't know why. You made me give up the horses and the lessons, which I shouldn't have had to do to begin with."

Adam cleared his desk with one sweep of his hand. "Do not turn this disgusting act of thievery on me. There is nothing that will compensate you breaking into my home, and there never will be. Do you have the combination to my safe?"

"How did you know?"

"I keyed in a safety code..."

"That tells you the number of times your program has been accessed. That's kindergarten computer stuff. I wasn't thinking," Sally responded. "I should have known your programs would be protected."

"Have you written the combination down anywhere? It must be destroyed."

Sally reached in her pocket and handed Adam the innocent-looking piece of paper. He grabbed it, slowly opened it up, and read the contents. His long, eerie silence compounded Sally's already unbearable nervousness. She cried in fear.

"Stop it. Do you think crying is going to make me change my mind about taking your speck of land away?"

"I don't know how you think you can do that, and I don't know what gives you the right—"

"A common thief talks of rights?"

"I wasn't going to steal from you. I just wanted to look at the disks."

"Go ahead then. Open the safe and look inside."

"No."

"I insist. I'll even open it up for you." Adam jerked aside the rug and turned the wheel of the safe. The door slammed on the floor.

Sally peered into the hole.

"Take the disks."

Sally sighed, weary from the battle. "I don't want to take them." She walked toward the window and stared upon the land that had given her the strength to fight for her dreams. The hills were far away, and the windmills were hidden in the midst of the dust, August's contribution to the landscape. Sally rubbed her eyes and turned away from the light. "I give up. I can't afford to live here. It costs too much."

"Your ranch was not worth—"

"So you think I am talking about the land?"

Adam closed the safe and sat in his chair, contemplating the situation. "Okay then, we'll be ranching partners. We'll make decisions together, equally, as to what goes on out there."

"Again with being partners? Well, that one has never quite worked, has it? One minute you are fighting me, the next you are joining forces with me again. I suppose partners have their riffs too."

"The choices about Karen affected me too. That child's father trusted me when I asked him if she could live with you. I feel very dishonest right now."

"I suppose it is the right thing to do. You have accomplished more on that land than I have."

"I'm glad you agree."

"I don't even know what I am agreeing to. Do I own the land or not?"

"I have work to do."

Sally drove away from the ranch slowly. She couldn't even remember how long it had been since she'd slowed down and enjoyed the scenery around her without feeling that sense of urgency to feed calves or check fences. Even though it was only the middle of August, Sally sensed that fall was in the air. She deliberately drove her vehicle along the roadside and stole the time to watch some leaves serenely drop from the scraggly Hackberry trees. Sally noticed the tall, leaning grasses bending under the strain of a practically rainless, Texas August, the relentless sun adding to the plants' burden in the pursuit of life. But among those tall reeds the colorful wildflowers were randomly dispersed, and, even though the grasses would eventually turn brown and die, the fields would never lose the color that grew beneath them. *Nature is sometimes wiser than humans,* Sally thought. When she reached her property, Chris and Karen were just pulling up to the fence, leaving the home the young fourteen-year-old had grown to love. Karen leaped from the truck and wrapped her arms around Sally as she was unlocking the gate.

"This has been the best summer of my whole life. Thank you." Sally smiled and held her tight.

"It was my best summer ever too," she whispered in the young girl's ear.

Duties on the ranch were performed mechanically for the next few weeks. Having to just feed the calves but not train or give lessons was a tremendous load off Sally's mind, and Chris did many jobs she didn't even realize had to be done to get the land ready to plant fruit trees. Sally enjoyed spending time with Al as she observed him eating, swishing his tail, and standing in the stock tank enjoying the cool water. Since she was officially a ranching partner with Adam, he sent Chris out daily to perform many of the ranch duties. Chris was a hard worker and a very nice young man. Since he had already graduated from high school a few months before, Sally knew he could stay indefinitely. He had no plans to attend college, as he said ranching was all he wanted to do in life.

Every night, Sally saddled up Lady Grace so that she could practice out in the fields. She had set up the barrels this time at the edge of her property. The sight was not visible to the house as her pastures gradually sloped downward so that the edge, when it reached the fence line, was remarkably lower than the land where the house was situated. Sally still felt driven to enter the competition at the Abilene rodeo, an accomplishment she could claim to be her own.

Sally had not visited her father or Aunt Lucille since Karen's departure. She thought about inviting them to the rodeo, but since everyone presumed she would not compete, Sally felt it simpler just to go on her own. Perhaps a different part of Texas would soothe her sullen demeanor.

The evenings in the house were quiet, something Sally would have to acclimate to, as Chris returned to the Hamilton Ranch each day after putting in ten hard hours on her place. She loved watching the windmill in the field through her window slowly stop turning as the evening hues eventually dominated the blue skies.

One late afternoon after Sally had fed the calves, she fixed herself something to eat and was perched at the table when Adam drove up and called her name. He opened the creaky screen door and silently stepped into the house, hat in hand.

Sally observed his movements in silence as he helped himself to some water from the refrigerator and then sat across from her, carefully placing the empty glass on the table. She scraped the plate as she stirred her food around in anticipation of the conversation to come.

"I said some things to you I regret."

"No need for regrets. I convinced a young girl that dishonesty was okay—something I've been preaching to you. Anyway, it was my battle. I should not have recruited soldiers."

"I've spoken with her father, and he bears no grudge. In fact, he said that Karen loved her summer and truly appreciates the friendship y'all developed. He worries about Karen not having a mother."

"I suppose I was like a mother to Karen, but I lost sight of what was important." Sally pushed her plate aside. "I can't seem to properly nourish any relationships here in Texas. I'm sure my dad and Lucille will eventually understand, but asking you to understand is a different story. Our relationship is a casualty in all of this, too many secrets, too many lies."

"Sally…"

"No. These evenings alone have afforded me the opportunity to think. I walk out to the windmill during the day and lean against the metal girders. I listen to the grinding and watch the shadows on the grasses jump as the wheel turns with the wind. Something I cannot even see moves metal in the sky. I plan on painting my visits one day when I understand them more." Sally rubbed her eyes, remembering the letters she so often read in New Orleans. "The fish in the pond surface as this metal structure aerates the water, allowing them to thrive as it steals the water from below the surface." She smiled at Adam, "Something I read in a letter once." Composing herself, Sally stated with confidence and conviction, "I still want my ranch. I still have aspirations. There's nothing wrong with that but not at the price of losing all the people who are closest to me. The irony here is I've lost something I never thought I had to begin with. I think you can want something so badly that you lose sight of the things that really matter in life, and that is friendship, trust, love. I've never shed so many tears in all of my life as I have this summer.

You know, I think I would welcome a Texas tornado or a plague of locusts in place of the emotions I've felt. I know those calves you sold me were special. It was obvious the first time I saw them. I also know you offered to give me Al again to take care of so I could have an income, and I know you put your name on my ranch so there will be some capital to operate and, you know, Adam, it doesn't feel so bad. Two months ago, I would have fought you tooth and nail, but being a partner or a part of things is okay. You've done a lot for me, Adam, and I will never forget our friendship and the brief passion that passed between us."

"There doesn't have to be an end..."

Sally rose and turned toward the window. "Yes, there does have to be an end. I know that."

Adam picked up his glass from the table, set it in the sink, and left the house.

The barrel-racing event Sally entered was scheduled during one of the Saturday night performances. Each evening there was a different group of entrants competing, keeping the seven-day rodeo interesting and diverse. There were, of course, the regulars who would perform every evening to please the loyal rodeo crowd. Sally explained to Chris she would be leaving Friday morning and would return Sunday afternoon, so he made arrangements to stay over at her place for two nights. She borrowed a pickup and horse trailer from the Straight S to load Lady Grace. If Chris wondered where she was going, he kept it to himself.

Sally hadn't spoken to any of her family or friends in weeks, with the exception of Adam's brief visit to her kitchen. Uncovering the truth was not her main driving force.

Sally left her small ranch minutes before Chris arrived at work. They passed on the road and she waved enthusiastically and yelled for him to take it easy while she was gone. She smiled to herself. Her small tract of land was running like clockwork thanks to both their expertise and she felt like she could really enjoy the trip and rodeo knowing Chris was there to look after the place. She drove along, enjoying the green cedars that dominated the hills and valleys.

Although farmers and ranchers immediately clear out any cedar trees because they suck the water from the land, their presence represents a life many people will never experience. The blue sky jetted into the horizon while the warm wind blew Sally's hair in and out of the truck. Lady Grace rode well in a trailer, so the trip was relatively stress free. Sally thought about the new shirt and jeans she purchased especially for the ride. She would finally shine and sparkle for about seventeen seconds.

Sally unloaded Lady Grace at the arena and accompanied her to a stall. After brushing and feeding the mare, Sally checked into her hotel, ate, and lay awake thinking only about her upcoming rodeo ride.

The next day, Sally practiced in the arena at her designated time, brushed down Lady Grace, and filled out more paperwork. She eyed her opponents keenly and knew the women she was competing against were skilled riders or they wouldn't have been there in the first place. Sally abandoned the practice area in plenty of time to dress and relax before the performance that evening.

Boisterous crowds poured into the coliseum around 6:30 p.m., and Sally had Lady Grace prepared for the event. Just having her cast removed two days earlier, she knew her arm would be a problem without the full dexterity needed to control the animal and guide her as close to the barrels as possible without tipping them over. The more experienced mares and geldings usually knew more than their human riders did, and Lady Grace's keen instinct would play a large role in the race. A fine horse was the key, and Sally patted Lady Grace on the neck, knowing she was on one of the best barrel racers in the state.

Sally's name and number reverberated over the loud speaker, and she nervously entered the chute waiting for the gate to fly open on her signal. The crowds cheered as the rodeo announcer read she hailed from the Straight S. Sally had totally forgotten that she had entered the competition before moving out onto her fifty acres. The fact that people were cheering for her because they thought she was a part of a massive and lucrative ranch—one that had made many important contributions over the years to the growth of Texas— instilled a sense of pride. The lighted board flashed a picture of the Straight S brand, and Sally knew losing was not an option. She was representing more than herself. The ride was short, her turns were smooth, and her time was excellent. Although she nervously waited for additional riders to finish, Sally sensed victory. She shared her happiness with the strangers in the crowd with a wave of her hat.

Sally drove onto her property early Sunday evening. Exhaustion enveloped her body, and Lady Grace stammered a bit in the horse trailer, anxious to be put out to pasture. Chris was in the middle of feeding the calves but temporarily stopped to help her unload the horse. He questioned the fact that there were no cows and she laughed, knowing he knew full well after seeing her with Lady Grace in the back of the trailer the day she left that she was headed to the rodeo. Sally reached in the truck and proudly showed off the first place ribbon and the check she'd received. She told him part of it was his for taking care of the ranch for two days all by himself.

As she gratefully walked into the house, Sally dropped her suitcase and plopped down on one of the wooden chairs. She propped her boot-clad feet up on a kitchen stool and threw her keys, ribbon, and check on the table. The rodeo had been exhilarating yet exhausting, a good diversion from her personal problems. A knock on the screen door interrupted her thoughts.

"Sally, can I come in?"

"Sure."

Adam took off his hat and sat down. "Where have you been?"

"I drove up to the rodeo in Abilene. You would have been proud of me. I won first place, sixteen seconds flat. It's not a record, but it was good enough to win, and I feel like a winner."

"That's great news! Congratulations. And your arm?"

"It's fine. The Straight S was credited for the ride. I forgot to tell them I wasn't a part of the ranch anymore."

"Sally, I have something to say that will make a difference in all of our lives, and I think you need to hear it. I think you'll want to hear it. Your aunt Lucille and father are waiting for us at the Straight S if you are up to going over there right now. I believe they realize you deserve to hear the whole truth. I'd like to join you, but if you'd rather do this alone, I'll understand."

Sally's boots hit the floor as she propped herself up in the chair. "It seems a lifetime ago that I was yearning for this moment. I don't know if I want to go or not. I've accepted the fact that my life is what I make it, and no one can take that away from me. I wonder why they want to tell me everything now."

"Perhaps they felt that losing you was too big a price for them to pay after all. Maybe they missed you while you were gone, thinking you may not return."

"I just went to the rodeo."

"Maybe you went farther than you think."

"Maybe so. Okay, I am ready, and yes, I'd like you to be there, like always."

"I'm glad you still noticed."

"I want to hear what they have to say, but for different reasons now."

As Sally and Adam drove over to the Straight S, he put his arm around her, attempting to dissipate the tension he knew she must be feeling. Sally smiled. She was reliving that sixteen-second ride at the rodeo.

John and Lucille were together on the couch while Adam and Sally each sat in an easy chair. Sally spoke first. "Before we begin, I just want to say it should have been me up in the attic looking in the trunk, not Karen."

Aunt Lucille looked at John, shook her head, and then cast her eyes downward almost as if in shame. Her father reached for Lucille's hand and squeezed it in a supporting manner. He viewed his tired daughter with empathy, a mirror image of the way he felt at the moment. Then, at last, the words that were so difficult, so impossible to verbalize all those years, suddenly became audible.

"Sally, it's been a long time since I've told the whole truth about my life to you or anyone around me. It hasn't been easy to support the weight of dishonesty over the years. It wears at you every day until you think it doesn't matter because you have nothing to lose in life anyway. Then you do lose something dear, and it is then that you realize only the truth is important, not the possible repercussions of your actions. I don't want to lose you or force you to become like me because I haven't been able to face the truth about my life."

Sally glanced sideways at Adam, but he was staring intently at John, his large fingers supporting his chin. Her father continued after shifting a bit and lovingly placing his arm around Lucille.

"I was only ten years old when I first began to work on the Straight S. I realized right from the start, even at such a young age, that I would never get to really know the cattle business without throwing myself into it, so I moved out to the ranch to work while I continued to go to school. It was in my blood, and I couldn't deny who I was. I worked harder and longer than any of the hands while I was there. I did all the tough jobs—the older hands saw to that—but I loved every minute of it. Every afternoon when I went home to the Straight S, I threw my schoolbooks down first thing and started to work in the barn or out in the fields or anywhere that involved ranching. I lived with all the hands and probably received more of an education doing that than I ever would have finishing school.

"The old man, Captain King, was hell, though, to work for at times." John stopped talking for a while, silently rehashing the past in his mind. Sally and Adam exchanged glances until John spoke up again. "But I had my fun too. There were get-togethers in town; we often drove to the movies and we entered all the rodeos around Benning, some even in Oklahoma. Then, one evening"—John sighed—"I met two of the prettiest girls in the county at one of the local barn dances. One of the young ladies was named Miss Laurel McCall and the other one was named Miss Lucille McCall. These two girls had only been nine and eleven years old when they were sent to live with their aunt after the death of their parents. They were raised and educated in Benning. I was twenty-five years old at the time, Laurel was eighteen, and Lucille was sixteen. I started out dating Laurel and we went out for several months before I realized Lucille was the one who held a place in my heart." John smiled. "Now, I'm going to stop there and start at the beginning of another story, and then you can see where the two will begin to meet.

"Listen to the whole story, honey." He glanced over toward the easy chair. "When Adam first realized that he needed to run for political office, I began to get a tad nervous. I knew him well enough and trusted him to boot, but there were secrets out there that I had and I didn't—couldn't—let be known until the death of your mother. There were sealed papers in Austin I had to keep sealed. I had already paid such a high price." He searched his daughter's eyes. "You already know, Sally, that Captain King was the original owner and founder of this ranch. He was a mean old codger and would stop at nothing to get his way. He had some mighty strange ways and some even stranger ideas. When he first began his life out here, way before the turn of the century, he had been too busy to marry and raise a family, or maybe no decent woman would move out in the middle of nowhere with that old cuss. I don't know. But when he realized he was up in years and had established a profitable ranch, he took on a real young wife and, within a year, she bore him a son. There were no more children, and all seemed to be going well as far as all of us knew until, out of the blue, about six years after the birth of the child, his wife just suddenly disappeared. No one knew where she disappeared to or why she left. Hell, the Captain was getting meaner and meaner as the years dragged on and more ruthless, if that was even possible. All of us hands at the ranch figured she ran off to get as far away from him as she could, but strangely enough she left the boy behind. Well, his son grew up on the ranch, the Captain thinking he would one day run the place and maybe even expand its boundaries into the next state. But the Captain didn't count on the child having the kind and sympathetic disposition he had obviously inherited from his mother. He was hard on the boy—almost cruel at times, trying to toughen him up for ranch life. Then, one day, just like the mother, the Captain's son was gone. He was only sixteen when he escaped his boundaries and it was anyone's guess as to where he disappeared to. Legend had it that he found his mother and lived with her until he married but we'll never know for sure."

John continued to speak slowly, his words burdened.

"Everyone knew the boy was ashamed of his father, Captain King, with his crooked dealings and cruel ways. One day the Captain received a letter from his son saying he could no longer bear his name and the reputation that superseded it. He denounced all ties to the ranch and his father and told him he was legally changing his surname to his mother's, a person who represented kindness and honesty. You know, King actually nailed that letter up on the wall in his house and would refer to it and slam it with his cane when he was angry with someone because of what he considered ultimate disloyalty. I remember it wasn't even readable hanging up there, but the Captain would quote from it often so all of us knew the letter by heart, especially those unfortunate enough to be the recipient of his wrath."

As though that was her cue, Aunt Lucille stood up and left the room. John was silent in her absence, pensive as he sat. She returned with a small, leather book in her hand and held it out to Sally.

"It's my mother's diary?" Sally asked, quietly taking the book.

"No. It's mine."

"Aunt Lucille, I don't want to read your diary."

"Yes, honey, you do. I was only sixteen years old when I began this book. There would be nothing in your mother's writings that could help you understand the past the way it should be understood. Go home now and take the book with you. When you've finished reading it, come back. Your father and I will be waiting and he will finish up his story when you return."

"Nothing that has happened in the past could change my love for the two of you," Sally said.

Lucille and John exchanged sad gazes.

"Come on, Sally. Let's go, okay?" Adam turned to John as he placed his arm around Sally. "I'm telling her everything, even what's between us." He then faced Sally. "Let's go back to my place. Chris is staying the night at your house."

For the first time in a long while, Sally found comfort on Adam's shoulder. He stroked her hair, lifting small strands repeatedly in a gentle, caring manner. "Adam, what did you say to my father to finally convince him to tell me the truth?"

"What someone should have said a long time ago. He agreed."

Sally and Adam entered the house and flipped on the lights. He left the living room and returned with two cups of coffee.

"Do you know what's in here?"

"Not all of it."

Sally opened the book and thumbed through the pages. "It's written in Aunt Lucille's hand. Do you mind if I read it aloud?"

"If that's what you want, but you certainly aren't obliged. I will wait for you here whether you read it aloud or not."

They both sat on the couch, shifting uncomfortably at first and then settling down. Sally cautiously opened the book and read the diary aloud. She noticed that each entry was filed under a day of the week instead of a date. Sally read aloud, her voice anxious.

"Sunday—My dearest diary, I am writing to you in a brand new book. You know I filled up the old diary with childish prattle, but now I am a young woman, sixteen, and Auntie gave me this as a gift for my birthday. So I will begin by telling you a most wonderful thing that has taken place in my life. It was yesterday, yet I can remember every detail like it was happening to me all over again today. It is almost too exciting for words, but I will try to find a way to tell you. Laurel and I met the most handsome young man from the Straight S last night, and we both danced with him. I think he was really kind of shy because at first he was very formal and asked if we had a father or someone at the dance so he could ask permission to even speak with us. Of course, we only had Auntie, and she said yes right away. He actually took turns dancing with only Laurel and me the whole night, and that was surprising because all those girls from town who go to the dances every Saturday night were there and dressed in those low-cut blouses that everyone seems to be wearing these days. But you already know that Auntie would never let Laurel and I wear such things. He told us good-bye with such eloquence I still swoon when I think about it. He took our hands, each one separately, and touched the back of our palms with his lips. It was not a kiss but a touch of romance that I shall remember all of my life. Then Auntie took us home, and I looked back at him while we were walking away and he smiled at me and bowed. Have you ever heard of anything so wonderful? Anyway, tomorrow I will find out more about him at school. I am going to ask everyone I know about him. I've decided I'm not going to describe him to you yet, diary; you will just have to be curious. You know it is my way of making you look forward to what I will tell you tomorrow. It is late, and I have a lot of thinking and dreaming to do.

"Monday—Today, I asked someone at school about John. That's his name. John McKenna. I don't think I told you that yesterday. I know I have never met anyone as romantic or as kind in all of my life. I have been thinking about him all day, and I just have to see him again. Laurel said she'd pick me up after she finishes work today to go into town. I am waiting now. I am already planning on how to get to see John again. I have to figure out a way for Laurel to take me to the Straight S so I can see him. She told me he was just a dirty old cattle puncher and that she wanted something better in life. Can you imagine, dear diary, someone better than John? After the way he said good-bye? But I am being very cruel to you, aren't I, because I haven't even described him to you yet. Have to go. Laurel is here at last, and she is honking impatiently, and it is me that has had to wait. Can you imagine?

"Tuesday—I know you've been dying to know what happened yesterday, and I shan't be unfeeling and make you wonder anymore. Laurel reluctantly took me over to the Straight S (I had to give her a dollar), and I saw John. He was standing on the porch talking to that old Captain King. It must have been the Captain's house because it is the best looking one out there. It has a big wraparound porch and is two-story, but the roof jets up to the sky almost as high as the windmills. The windows are large and have shutters on either side of them. It is a strong, dark house. But I am not writing to tell you about an old house. I am writing to tell you about John. He is so tall. (You probably already guessed that.) I have to tilt my head up to him when I speak. He wears a hat all the time, and he is very rugged looking. Diary, should I admit it? I am very attracted to him. He eyes are the bluest I've ever seen, and I could brush my hands all day through his hair. I am afraid I am telling you too much. But I know you would never reveal my secrets to anyone. I can't wait until I see him again, because all we did was pass by him in the car. But I know I will be counting the minutes until I get to see him again. I'm afraid I have lost my heart already as Auntie said I would do one day. I didn't know it would be this fast. Good-bye, dear diary! I am so happy!"

Sally looked up at Adam. "Your house used to belong to Captain King…and the windmills…" Sally continued reading.

"Wednesday—Oh, dear diary, I'm afraid I have horrible news. I am surprised that I have not died already from grief. Auntie found out we went over to the Straight S yesterday and was furious with us. She said we couldn't ride out there anymore because that old Captain King was crazy and no telling what he'd do if he found out that two single girls had visited his place for no good reason. But life is so confusing because why did Auntie let me dance with John if now I can't even see him? Life can be so cruel. I have been crying a lot today. I'm afraid I am worrying Auntie. But I can't help it. Laurel says I am just a twit, but I know better. Hopefully I will write something happier tomorrow. I do not feel like sitting here any longer. You'll just have to wait.

"Thursday—Dear diary, I hope you have a long time to listen today. Please be patient with me while I tell you what happened. Most of it I don't even understand myself; maybe you can figure it out. When I got home from school yesterday, guess who was in our living room? No, I know you think it was John, but it wasn't. It was that old Captain King. He must be at least a hundred years old. He looks like it anyway. He was arguing with Auntie about something and their voices were real loud, and when they saw me, they both got very quiet and Captain King left right away. I asked Auntie what it was all about, and she mumbled something about how crazy he was and that it wasn't my concern. But then she said something wonderful. She told me John was invited over to dinner tomorrow night. I asked her why he was coming, and she said he was a nice young man and could come over anytime he wanted. Isn't that wonderful, diary? I am going to have to put my hair up, because as you know I look older that way. I wonder if it will matter that I am only sixteen and he is already twenty-five? Do you think it matters, dear diary? Does age make a difference? Well, this time it won't, I will be sure of that. I am also going to wear my black, full skirt. It makes me look like I have hips already. Oh diary, how will I even manage to eat? But I must, or he will think I'm a twit like Laurel says. I shall hardly be able to keep my mind on my studies. I have always loved Friday company, but this time I'm afraid I will want to pray it never ends. That's not bad, is it, diary? I have to go to help Auntie with the dishes. She has called me twice already. Life is so good. Bye!

"Friday—Can't write much today, diary, I have to get ready for tonight. Wish me luck!

"Saturday—How can a person be so sad, diary? After I dressed up, helped with dinner, put my hair in a French curl, and I wore makeup, John asked Laurel out after dinner, and she said yes. She told me he was just a cowpuncher, and now she has agreed to go out with him. I can't stand it. I have cried all day, and Auntie asked me if I was sick. Oh yes, dear diary, love sick! But I couldn't say that, so I told her I didn't do well on a test at school on Friday. I hated to lie to her, but she would have treated me like a child if I had told her the truth. She said not to worry about the test. Life goes on. But it doesn't feel as though it will go on for me. Dearest diary, what shall I do?

"Sunday—I hate my sister. She gloated to me she had a wonderful time with John last night. How can it be? I know you'll think I am foolish, but I know I love him already. I know it in my heart, dear diary. And now, Laurel is going on a picnic with him today. I have bad news for you. I hope you don't hate me for it, but I have decided I will not write to you anymore, dear diary, until I am happy once again. If it turns out that I am never to be happy again, then this will be my last entry. I love you, diary. Good-bye."

Sally stopped reading and thumbed through blank pages. "She left pages and pages empty. I guess my mom and dad were dating all that time." Sally looked at the book and sipped on her coffee nervously. "Here's the next entry."

"Sunday—I have missed you, dear diary, but I didn't want you to be sad like me and I know you would have been, had I written to you these past months. I will try to catch you up on everything as best I can. For I feel, at last, I have good news. First of all, John and Laurel have been dating for the past four months. I avoided seeing John, as I could not even think of them together. My heart would have ached too much. But Auntie was getting tired of my moods and wanted me to get out of the house, so she made John and Laurel take me to the Winter Carnival. During the dance, Laurel felt sick, and John took her home. He came back though to the carnival and danced with me, only me, all night. I thought I had died and gone to heaven. After the dance he took me home right away, because Auntie would worry. But he asked me if he could pick me up from school on Monday. Since Laurel does not like to pick me up anyway, I didn't think it would be a problem. I cannot tell you how elated I am, dear diary. My prayers have truly been answered. After months of thinking I would never live again all of a sudden John has paid some attention to me instead of Laurel. I am so happy that it scares me to write it down, like I might be cursing my happiness or something. Do you believe in curses, dear diary?

"Monday—John picked me up from school today, and the joy I felt in my heart was indescribable. Have you ever felt, diary, that you would never be truly loved or truly love before you died? I used to feel that way, but now I can tell you I don't think that way anymore. I truly love John, and I know he feels the same. He told me all his inner thoughts and desires today. He has such strong ambitions and goals. Perhaps that is why I love him so. He knows what he wants and goes after it. He told me he has been working for the Straight S for fifteen long years and that Captain King says one day it could all be his. Can you imagine? John owning the Straight S? I know he will run the ranch well, diary, but I had to ask why the Captain would choose him and not a relative? He told me the Captain's son ran away and that John had been loyal to him all these years. He said he rewarded loyalty. John constantly talks and talks about his love for the land. It is as though he gathers strength from it. It is what he lives for. It is his goal to be the owner of the Straight S, and I know I will be there beside him one day when that happens."

Sally looked up at Adam. "My God, my father and I are so much alike. It is scary."

"Something I've noticed." Adam smiled.

"Tuesday—John picked me up again today after school. He said he needed to tell Laurel he wasn't going to date her anymore. I know Laurel will be angry because no one has ever told her no before or rejected her. And to think it will be for me. That sounds vain, but I can't help it. It is like I told you before—I am loved for myself, and I truly love John in return. Our happiness is found here in Texas, and all Laurel ever talks about is leaving Texas and having money and influence. Maybe some day she'll realize it is right under her nose. But I'm glad she is not with John anymore. She was not good for him. Diary, we went to the Straight S and watched the windmills under the stars last night. They turned even in the gentle breeze, and I could hear the scraping sounds of the metal as they went around and around endlessly. John kissed me, and I felt so good I had tears in my eyes. We both laughed, but I could tell it touched John's heart, for his kisses do move me so."

Sally stopped reading. "The more she fell in love with my father, the more picturesque her writings became. It was as though he inspired her." Sally continued to read page after page of Lucille's love for John and his in return for her. She read about windmills and sunsets, her writing poetic and touching, just like the letters she had written Sally under the guise of her mother. It dawned on her now how she was able to describe the land so well and Sally's mind reeled back to the beginning of summer when she had discovered the land her aunt often wrote about on Adam's ranch. Lucille had spent a whole year of her life out there with her father talking about dreams and goals and ambitions. Sally read about her father's incredible desire for the land, Aunt Lucille skillfully conveying his passion in her writings. The diary went on for a year before there was a day when something wasn't written. About a month's worth of pages were blank and then Sally read what she had been waiting so long to hear.

"Saturday—My dear diary, I have not written in such a long time because my heart was and still is in such turmoil. They say for the happiest time in everyone's life, there is an equal sadness. It is true. Laurel did not take being rejected by John so lightly. In the year's time John and I were dating she found out things I didn't even dream existed. My sister knows how to get her way, and one month ago she came into my room and told me she had been over to see Captain King many times during the past year. She said there had always been rumors about her and me in town. There had been since we moved here. She told me I was always such a happy little twit that I never noticed how people talked about us. My last name, diary, as you know, is McCall. Laurel said the Captain's wife's name was McCall before they married. She said they had a son who had run away and changed his name to his mother's maiden name because he could not bear his father's cruelty or accept the things he had done in the past to get what he wanted. Auntie's name was McCall before she married. Don't you see, dear diary, Laurel and I are the grandchildren of Captain King and Auntie is his wife's sister. We are the children of the son who ran away from his dishonesty and cruelty. I found out from Laurel that when our parents died we were sent here to live with our only living relative on my mother's side. That is what the Captain and Auntie were arguing about that day. I don't think he was even sure who we were until he and Auntie argued. And now he truly likes Laurel, because she has been loyal to him. He sees himself in her. She conspired against me, and to think it was me that wished she knew what was right under her nose. Laurel and the Captain have plotted against me. I don't stand a chance. They have a bond, now, and the Captain told John he was to marry Laurel and then, upon the Captain's death, provided they stayed married, John would inherit the ranch. No one could know the truth, or the contract would be void. That was Laurel's idea. Didn't I tell you she was vain? It is her way of keeping John forever and saving face. She doesn't want the town to know John is being forced to marry her. She could never stand the shame. She wanted John and she got him, and she wants to be sure he will never leave her. She is strong-willed like the Captain and will produce strong children, not weak ones like his wife did. That is what she said to him. She told me that is how she convinced him to go along with her. I would have produced weak, kind children with John. The Captain told Laurel that he finally got his revenge over his son, because the ranch would still be kept in the family. Dear diary, I am part of the family, but a weak part, so the Captain prefers Laurel. I should be the one at his side when the Straight S is finally his."

Sally let the last entry sink in. "Adam, my father owns the Straight S..." She was silent as the implications sunk in. "But he gave up Lucille. How could he do that?"

"The same way any of us are willing to give up everything to get what we want."

"But why didn't Dad say anything to me after Mom died? Why did he continue to keep it a secret that he owned the ranch?" Not really expecting an answer, Sally flipped through the pages and continued to read aloud, her voice faltering a bit under the strain.

"Saturday—Dear diary, I know it has been a long time since I've written. I love John so much that I'm afraid I have to give him up so he can truly be happy and have his dreams come true. If he marries Laurel, he can have everything he's worked so hard to achieve. Under the circumstances, Auntie said she is sending me to New Orleans to a young ladies' school on the outskirts of town. I know the Captain is helping her do this. I know I shall never love again, but I must leave something with John to remember me by. I am crazy with sadness and anger. I am not thinking straight, and I told Laurel everything. She told the Captain. They are hateful to me, diary, and have made me promise the most horrible thing. They have everything planned out, and think the money they send will compensate for my unhappiness. I know John would try to stop me from going if he found out, especially now, so I must not tell him my plans. I know now why the Captain wants somebody like Laurel to marry John. She will stop at nothing to get what she wants. I guess I am a twit, just like Laurel has always said. Good-bye."

Sally sat with tears in her eyes. "She loved him so much she gave him up. I wonder if my mother ever really loved him over the years." She looked at Adam. "I feel so sorry for my father. I have so many questions."

"I can answer some."

"Why didn't anyone know that my aunt Lucille was the one who really loved my dad?"

"It was like it said in the diary. Your father did not tell anyone because that was part of the agreement, at Laurel's insistence. She was afraid your father might leave her in the future, so no one was to know John owned the Straight S until after the death of either one of them. That was the information in that sealed packet in Austin. The Captain had drawn up papers to ensure dual ownership on the ranch, for the public eye, a corporation; the sealed contents contained the information that your father was the sole owner of the Straight S under some pretty sick terms. It was only to be opened if the agreement set by your mother was broken. You see, Laurel knew she had to have a hold over John all those years. If he left her or if anyone found out he owned the ranch, in the legal papers Captain King had drawn up, the Straight S would no longer be his. It was a sick hold she had over your father purely for vanity. That is why your dad panicked when the government sent out those letters denying the subsidies. There surely would have been an investigation and at that point your mother was still alive, and then Mr. and Mrs. Wright found out… Anyway, Laurel knew she could not live with the humiliation of everyone knowing your father loved Lucille instead of her; she also knew that if your father was recognized publicly as legal owner of the ranch, there would be a chance he would leave her. So she made up the stipulation, and the Captain had it sealed. John owned the ranch all those years, and then again he didn't. Laurel had to have control, just like the Captain. I guess she inherited all those ruthless characteristics from her grandfather, but it is ironic that she wanted all that power and money but under her own conditions had to live as a foreman's wife all her life. She couldn't see that everyone was a loser in a situation like that." Adam sighed.

"It was five years ago when you were sent off to college that your mother became adamant about telling everyone the truth. Perhaps all that time of knowing John didn't really love her finally sent her over the edge. She knew she hadn't all that long to live and by telling everyone and knowing John could not inherit would be her final revenge. But if she did tell everyone the truth, then all those years John put in would have been for nothing. He began to sell the land to me, little by little, under the ownerships of the ranch hands. He was afraid he could not stop your mother and so he wanted to preserve as much of the land as he could, in the hands of a friend, he said. He didn't want it back, claimed he had already paid a big enough price for it. That's why he parceled out the acreage titles under so many names. The original lawyer who handled all the paperwork for the Straight S died, and his son inherited his firm. He lived up north. Your father figured the son would never suspect any unusual dealings since he lived so far away until he moved down here.

"Wright?" Sally asked, astonished. "So when he worked at the county office to record name changes he found out a lot of information. He also was privy to the contracts left to him by his father."

"Yes, at first he asked me questions that I admit made me nervous, but I bought the land free and clear with your father's blessing. There was nothing in the agreement that said your father could not do with the land what he wanted. He just didn't tell Laurel about it. Wright got to know Tans because his name was on a section of the deeds. I suppose two crooked people together figured they had an opportunity to get something for nothing." Adam stood up, moved by the scene outside the window. He watched the prairie's movements while the clouds passed over the moon. "In response to your comment, yes, my house used to be a part of the Straight S many years ago. You don't remember it because after your father married Laurel he had the smaller house built. He refused to live in King's home with Laurel knowing how he felt about Lucille and all the good times they had spent there. I'm sure that's why you don't even remember it being part of the Straight S. This house and the land around it was one of the first sections John sold to me. My father and mother's original house burned about two years ago when a tornado tore through the ranch.

"You and my father have had many personal talks over the years," Sally said sadly, realizing that she had never had such intimate conversations with her own dad.

Adam turned and smiled. "You weren't here."

"I suppose. Anyway, I can see why you were so nervous about those deeds and the disks. Not knowing if the Texas laws even recognized the Straight S as legal to begin with must have been tough to handle for both you and my father. Another good reason you sought representation in Austin. So Captain King doubled his tracks. He had a lawyer hold the contract for him, and, in case that wasn't enough, he bought a judge's favor and placed another copy of the contract under sealed records attaching strict stipulations. He was very clever... I can understand everything I have read in the diary and everything you have explained to me, and the love between Aunt Lucille and my father, but why wouldn't Dad have told everyone after Mother died? He had a right. It would have been a perfect time to get everything out in the open when I returned from New Orleans, or even when I discovered that Aunt Lucille and my father were in love. Why didn't he tell me? That is the part I don't understand."

Adam turned once again toward the window and ignored her question. "You notice that the Straight S lives up to its name when it's combined with part of the Hamilton Ranch. The hills shape the S curves toward the sky and the ground boundaries are straight."

"So the two ranches are not really complete until they are joined together." He sat back down on the couch beside Sally.

"I suppose you can look at it that way."

Sally felt numb. She had been reading for a couple of hours, Adam listening intently to every revealing word. "You own my property, don't you? It was you that sold it to me, all those good grasses and well-kept fields at such a low price, and before that, it was a part of the Straight S."

Sally picked up both coffee cups and went into the kitchen to refill them. She returned and rubbed her neck as she sat beside Adam once again. She carefully picked up the diary and held it in her hands. "You know, I still don't understand why Aunt Lucille had to leave. I could tell by her letters that she loved this land too. Surely, something could have been worked out. Although, now I'm sounding disloyal to my mother. I loved my mother very much." She began to cry and flip through the pages. "There is no more."

"Sally…"

"Why would Mom want to tell everyone the truth after all those years?"

"Maybe it was the ultimate revenge when she finally realized that she couldn't control a situation she had given up her life for. I think she knew she couldn't have children when she married your dad…"

"She had me," Sally said simply.

"No. She didn't."

And right then is when Sally knew what John had revealed to Adam at the hospital.

Chapter Nine

Please don't let them take it down.
It's been there for so long.
I've always known its presence.
I've always heard its song.

"Don't worry, child." The farmer laughed
"The windmill will not turn.
It's served its time upon this farm.
A new song you will learn."

There was emptiness up in the sky.
I had an empty heart.
I wanted back my windmill.
The farmer could have made it start.

Soon I saw the old replaced.
A silver, sleek new windmill's song—
I heard its voice outside my room.
I hummed the whole day long.

Sally opened up the screen door slowly, allowing it to shut lightly while restraining the handle with her hand. She stepped into the living room of her father's house. Lucille and John were sitting together on the couch drinking coffee. "I'm surprised you're not outside on the porch. There is a nice breeze coming up from the south," Sally said quietly.

Lucille looked warily at John and then at Sally. "You know everything?"

Sally sat in one of the easy chairs. "Yes. Adam filled me in on the details." She stared at the two of them helplessly. "I cannot believe through all the years I lived here, I didn't even have the slightest hint of what was going on. I am so amazed that I don't even have a reaction at this point, only questions, and I really already know most of the answers," Sally spoke with exhaustion in her voice. "Dad, I don't know where to begin. I guess a lot of things make sense now. I know why you didn't want me out there on my own land. Not only was it because I would one day own the Straight S but it was because I reminded you of yourself twenty-two years ago.

"God, Sally, I didn't want you to live your life like I did, to be driven by a force of having to acquire something no matter what the cost. I've paid for my mistakes for twenty-two years. Lucille has too. You were so adamant in what you wanted, and nothing was going to stop you. Adam decided to keep his distance when I told him about Lucille the day at the hospital; he made it perfectly clear he didn't like being dishonest with you for any reason anymore. I put him in the middle of things more than once, and that was wrong. But he finally convinced me we were all headed for disaster at the rate we were going. When deceit is involved, there is no easy way out. I transferred those deeds to my ranch hands' names for the subsidy, and then I panicked when Wright approached me, making it clear he knew my secret. Then Tans started making waves about keeping the land, and that's when I knew I had to sell parcels to Adam just in case."

"Dad, it's like you've never known peace your whole life, but you were so willing to watch me struggle and search for the truth."

"Don't you see, Sally? You were an exact copy of me when I was young. You were willing to do anything to get what you wanted, and what did it get you? The same thing it got me. The people I truly cared about were pushed aside for my desires. I was watching you go through all the motions just as I had. I wanted to tell you the truth, but I was a coward. Then Lucille came back into my life, and even she couldn't convince me to face my past, to face the truth about you.

I thought I was ready when your mother told me she was going to finally tell everyone about the whole situation. I became so angry. I told her I didn't care about the land anymore, but she wasn't going to hurt you. That's when I insisted you go to Lucille's house. She did have feelings for you, honey, in her own way. I want you to always know that. She ultimately proved it by letting you go. Her need for revenge rested with me. I was the one who could never give her what she wanted. I have gone over the events of my past every day for twenty-two years, standing out on that porch and asking myself if it was all worth it. I have to tell you it was not. I had no one to share my love with." He pulled Lucille closer to him. "I would have given it all up for her, but she wouldn't let me, and then again, I have to ask myself if I didn't let her go a bit too easily, putting my interests first."

Lucille spoke up quickly. "No, John, I would never have come back as long as I knew there was a chance you could have lost the ranch." Lucille looked to Sally. "I left out so much in those diaries. Your father's feelings, Sally, were so sincere. If you could have heard him talk about the land and what it meant to him."

The implication of what her aunt was telling her tore through Sally's heart. "And so you chose my father's feelings over mine."

John rose to Lucille's defense. "Sally, don't blame—"

"Don't blame who? Are you talking about my mother, Laurel, or my mother, Lucille?" Sally cried at last. "I don't know what to feel. I don't know how you felt when you handed me to her sister." She directed her words at Lucille. "I was a pawn."

"It wasn't like that, Sally. I wanted you to have everything, to have every advantage. Captain King had power. You have to understand; there was no law out here except his law. He promised to make life very difficult for you and me. This way, you were raised with a legacy and your father. The other way you would have had just a mother who was sick with sadness all the time, one who wasn't strong enough to fight back." She looked at Sally sadly. "When I found out I was pregnant with you I couldn't believe it. I was so happy. I thought it would make everything right. Surely Captain King would change his mind now, I told myself. But I was looking for humanity where none existed. I thought even he wouldn't be so cruel as to not let John and me be together under the circumstances. But I was a naïve fool. It didn't make any difference to him. He wanted John and Laurel to marry, and nothing would stop him, not even when it involved the life of an innocent unborn baby. He said it was best for you. He told me to do it for John, that if I really loved him, I would let him raise his baby on a ranch that might one day be his." She grabbed John's arm. "Your father didn't even know I was pregnant until you were born." Lucille squeezed his hand and stared at Sally. "Captain King died on the night you were born. But the contracts were all made up… He even had the courts on his side. You inherited your great-grandfather's iron will, but you also inherited your great-grandmother's kindness and compassion. You're a fortunate woman."

"I don't feel very fortunate right now. In fact, I feel pretty empty. Perhaps Adam was right. Sometimes the truth should just stay in the past." Sally rubbed her forehead and aching eyes. "I feel so tired. I just want to go home and sleep." She tapped the diary on her palm and relinquished the book back to its rightful owner. "Here. I know you'll want to keep this." Sally walked out the door and into the truck, where Adam was waiting. He turned off the radio when Sally slid into the seat.

"Are you all right?"

"I don't know. Are there any more secrets that I could possibly find out about before morning? Please, just take me home."

"Let's go back to my place tonight. I don't want to leave you alone."

Sally nodded and gazed out the window through tear-filled eyes. She fell asleep, her arm providing a cushion as she rested it on the open window. At home Adam covered Sally with a sheet after he kindly placed her on the bed. He sat in an easy chair beside her, propping his feet and laying his head back against the soft cushions. There were too many things on his mind right now, and he wished he too could fall asleep and close the world out for a while. He focused on Sally's shallow breathing while inwardly complimenting the loveliness of her face at peace. Adam was in love with Sally and had known this fact for a long time. "It may never happen now," he whispered to the night as he turned and gazed at the windmills.

Sally woke up right before sunrise immediately noticing Adam asleep, slumped in the chair beside the bed, his weathered hand supporting his chin. She observed him for a while and then suddenly realized how Lucille felt about her father. Sadness captured her heart at first only to be quickly replaced by a lingering tranquility as she quietly headed toward the window. The windmills were still; they were not speaking yet. "Tell me what to do," she beckoned to the horizon.

Adam woke and moved behind her as the sun slowly expanded the sky. They each chose to follow their hearts with no regrets.

Adam left the house to the everyday noises of cattle, tractors, and loud voices. Sally searched for a clock on the wall and decided she would also have to dress and head back to her land. Even though Chris was there, she knew it was her responsibility to oversee the calves, the horses, and Al. Sally constantly thought of Lucille and how she must have felt. She thought of the diary and words Lucille wrote, "for every happy moment in life there is an equally sad one." Sally thought of the heartache Lucille must have gone through, and her father too. In an instant she decided that she must visit her mother and father right away.

Chapter Ten

Please let me show you the remnants of my youth.
Let me tell you stories of ethics and of truth.
Let me tell you where to go, let me tell you where to lie,
Upon the grass-filled ground beneath the heated sky.

Let me love you and assist you in all you try to learn,
Let my past be of assistance, let my passions in you burn.
Let my tales and jokes and blatant woes guide you on
your way.
Let my retreat of youth lure you when you need a place
to stay.

Let me convince you of your fortune to live on Texas land,
The place beneath the windmills where you always
make a stand.
Let me show you life's escape beneath the shadowed sky,
Basking in serenity watching wild birds fly.

Sally knocked a few times on the screen door of her father's house
and entered when she heard voices and clanking of dishes emanating from the kitchen. She stopped at the entry and observed Lucille
and her father laughing and touching each other lovingly. It was
a pleasant sight, but Sally instantly looked to the floor, feeling as

though she was invading their privacy. She could not ever remember John looking at Laurel in such a way or touching her.

Lucille noticed Sally awkwardly standing in the doorway and enthusiastically invited her to join them for breakfast. She agreed and helped set the table, imitating a normal family. They all sat down, each a bit nervous with the situation, but, after a while, Sally realized she enjoyed the company of two parents who openly loved each other. Her dad confidently expressed his feelings while he laughed and showed affection toward Lucille constantly, touching her hand as she passed a dish or bending to the side and kissing her on the cheek in between bites of food. After her own experience that morning, Sally realized that Lucille and her father had missed out on so much in life.

"I have something to tell you," Sally finally announced. John and Lucille held hands as she spoke. "I want you to know that I have thought about all of these revelations for only a short while but have come to the conclusion that we all do what we feel is right at the time. I have found someone in my life, and I know how you must have felt, Aunt Lucille, when you fell in love with my father. Both of you have suffered for many years because of the effects of someone with so much blind power that he actually thought he could rule lives. But you have proven him wrong, and I am so happy for you." Sally reached for her father's hand. "Dad, after waiting all these years, it would be wrong of me not to acknowledge and support your right to love Lucille and own a ranch you worked so hard for and gave up so much for. It would be like me playing the Captain's role all over again. I know now why my mother wasn't ever interested in the things I liked to do and why Aunt Lucille and I got along so famously in New Orleans. The truth of the matter is, sitting here watching you two has made me realize that I like having two parents who love each other, and now it is my turn to carve my place in the world with a little bit more wisdom than most start out with, thanks to you. I love you both."

On the way back to her ranch, Sally felt at peace. The memory of Lucille's kind face as she left the house would be imprinted in her mind for the rest of her life. Sally smiled.

Sally was still engrossed in her thoughts and didn't realize Adam had driven up behind her as she began to unlock the gate. He grabbed her and held on tight as the ranch that lay in front of them sprang alive with horses galloping toward the trough for morning oats, Al romping with the other calves as the horses stirred them into motion, and the windmills beginning their daily ritual.

They kissed and returned to their vehicles. Sally yelled from the window, "Thanks for leaving me the keys to the truck this morning! I'll have Chris return it this afternoon."

"Chris won't be coming out today."

"I suppose we'll figure out a way to get it back later then."

After carefully checking out Al and the other calves, Adam and Sally, hand in hand, strolled back to the house. They lay in bed beside each other for a while, silent and content, until the ranch again stirred them to duty.

Sally fixed lunch and placed their plates on the table in the kitchen. Adam spoke first. "I seem to remember at one of our last meetings that you felt this relationship of ours was not going to survive."

"You have a way of reviving ailing hearts," she said, placing two glasses of iced tea down and sitting across from him.

"Sally, I don't want to make the same mistakes your father and mother made."

"I like the way that sounds—my father and mother."

"You are all right about that?"

"I would be the loser if I wasn't." Sally thought about how the fulfillment of her own relationship with Adam forced her to empathize what her father and Lucille must have gone through to be separated all those years.

"We almost followed the same pattern as they did, you know. Promise me there will never be one more word of dishonesty or deceit between us."

"I promise."

Adam drank his tea and pushed his chair away from the table. "I had to see your father about some business this morning. That's where I went when I left the house."

"We must have just missed each other over there."

"Twice. I had to go back again a second time so he could give me a copy of this month's *Texas Stockman*." Adam retrieved the magazine from his jacket pocket and set it on the table. "He mentioned you came over this morning."

"We had a nice breakfast, the three of us."

"You bring a great deal of joy to your father. I suppose you've made life bearable for him all these years." Adam smiled. "You know your little place is doing well, Sally. I am surprised the fields are still green. Putting in that extra fence and rotating the livestock really made a difference. Those calves are flourishing. The bulls will bring a good price in the spring. You might even make fifty cents this year."

Sally laughed. "You are awful!"

"Actually, it's a compliment. No one makes a profit the first year, especially with this tiny bit of land. You really have an instinct for this kind of work. You've done a fine job."

"Thanks."

"You know, Chris has been taking good care of this place for you."

"For *us*, partner."

"I thought maybe it would be nice if he could start out his life with a house and a few acres of flourishing land."

"What are you trying to say?"

"I gave him this property as a graduation present."

"But he is only seventeen years old!"

"Seven years older than your father when he started out."

"But this is mine…ours."

"We'll have plenty left, especially when the collaboration of the two ranches is complete."

"What collaboration?"

"I told you I talked over some business with your father this morning. We decided to join the two ranches together and make a go of it as partners. Besides, the ranches are so intertwined now, neither one of us is willing to sort it out. In addition, four names on the deed to a ranch this large will be advantageous."

"Four names?"

"Yeah. Four equal partners: John McKenna, Lucille McKenna, Adam Hamilton, and, if you agree, Sally Hamilton."

"Of course I agree!" Sally hugged Adam. "I am so happy." There is one more thing I think you need to know…"

"No. I don't want to hear any more secrets…"

Adam placed his hand over her mouth and whispered in her ear. "You were the best rider at that rodeo. You have to wear that outfit again for me sometime."

Sally hugged Adam effusively. "You were there!"

"We're going to be partners," he said.

"I thought we already were."

"This time on paper."

Sally and Adam kissed as the *Texas Stockman* fell to the floor with Al's picture on the cover and, in the background, the windmills, standing, quietly waiting for the sun.